LOUIS THE

The Search for

By

AJ Howard

Illustrations are in black and white

1st Edition

Made in the USA

With Thanks:

To all rodents for their lovely faces and curly whiskers.

With Special Thanks:

Dr Ian Howard, my brother, thank you for all your assistance in making this novel successful in a beastly market. Thank you for your advice and commitment to the task, I could not have done it without you. Thank you for giving me the confidence to continue in my writing.

Cliff Cooper-Liles, thank you for grammatical assistance through various stages in the completion of this 1st edition, although I did ignore some of your squeaking.

Publisher information: with thanks to Amazon
Charleston, South Carolina, USA, 2011

subtitle Travels of a Donkey* used on next page as main title may offend

Grammatically written in UK English

fatmousestudios.com

Louis the Furred series continues

III - Angels with Dirty Whiskers

Other kids stuff

Warthogs

Fat Mouse presents series

Other stuff by AJ Howard

Travels of a Donkey*

The Asylum Years

Ten Stories High

Jimmy Riddle

Contents: **Page**

4 Sacred Scroll Riddles each with 6 chapters

Pour away your emotion and hunt in this wood, for it is the things we do today that will be remembered that are good

When there is no movement and instincts take command, the truth may hurt but answers will be found

***Russian Roulette - One false move you may regret**

A spy will open closed eyes -
He makes the world seem bigger, yet he is much smaller

***Note from the Author:**

The creation of a written **Mouse code** sound without a solution would be, I feel, unjustified. Therefore the Wingding3 font shapes were used for some of the Russian Roulette chapters. These taps and scrapes can be translated, but are not similar to Morse code.

The full English alphabet translates in **two** versions:

Lower case:

a b c d e f   g h i j k l m   n o p q r s t   u v w x y z

⇨⇦⇨⇦⇨←   →↑↓↖↗↙↘   ↔↕▲▼△▽◀   ▶◁▷◣◢◤

Higher case:

A B C D E F   G H I J K L M   N O P Q R S T   U V W X Y Z

↳⇠⇢⇆⇵⇋   ⇵⇇⇉⇈⇊↶↷   ↪⮌↻↺⟲⌅^   ⌥␣ ␣⇪⇪⇦

<u>An example:</u>

These shapes and arrows translate to spell **Louis the Furred**

↶↕▶↓▽ ◀↑⇨ ⇋▶△△⇨⇦

Key to Creatures:

MICE	HAMSTERS	RATS	CROSSBREEDS
Louis	Andrew	Potty	Richard
Jane	Ken	Fruitcake	Paul
Max (the Professor)	the Collective	Truly Bonkers	Jerbil MacTaggart*
Eon	MacDrid*	Crazy*	Howard*
Jim	DaVid	Barmy	Crimson

Unpredictables	Humans
Scratchers	Cats
Round Faces	Owls
Woofers	Dogs

The Ssssylfia	Manifestation
Black and White Scratcher	Colin
Ginger Scratcher	Grimley

*these creatures appear from Volume Three onwards

INTRODUCTION

Hello, I'm **Jane** your narrating mouse. Times have changed for us. Our dreams have become bigger and our quests have become fulfilling. I think I am happy. I am free from that horrid bird-shaped prison and I roam the underground tunnels of London with my friends. Louis has been a true leader in a lot of ways. His vision of escape has been, so far, exciting. It's been a funny few days. Not funny in the sense that I've been laughing and joking. It has been a weird, somewhat odd time. Firstly, we lost Eon. Then we discovered Jim is the enemy to hamsters. We've had unpredictables scare us, scratchers chase us, round faces hunt us and yet we are alive. We've met intelligent rats and the Ssssylfia, that odd ghost. We've discovered magical routes by fortune rather than by skill. I now believe many of the Sacred Scrolls are myths rather than the truth but as we progress we are now searching for the meaning of Dark Energy. We at last have a mission, but only time will tell if it can be solved.

Louis is a military-style mouse. He has been an asset in our struggle to find our true selves. I think he does however believe too much in the Sacred Scrolls. It is all too easy to go by the rules, plod along and accept everything that is written must be correct. This is his weakness. We are following our dream to become great, free mice and yet in a way we are being held up by his downright pig-headed attitude. Don't get me wrong, if it wasn't for him we'd still be stuck in that sawdust prison still bored and wondering what the world had in store for us. I just feel his leadership is becoming weak. Louis keeps on that he is the leader. He says this is Louis' World and we all agreed to it. He says our next mission is to find Eon, yet it is obvious to everyone else that Eon does not want to be found. Yes, Louis spoke to the notorious white flakes; he negotiated with a group of hamsters, killed or at least injured the evil Andrew Archdeacon and risked everything to speak with the Sacred Lamb. He is a great mouse. I don't hate him, but his methods are somewhat foolish.

Max, or the Professor as he likes to be called, is a funny old mouse. He fulfilled part of his ambition when he ran across the grass at Clapham Common. He is a selfish creature though. He says he is a Professor and invented little white tablets that use imagination and desire to work. It made me laugh when he asked me to design a Max-Sub with my imagination and it looked like a pig, powered by an old bicycle! It must be a truly wonderful thing to be an inventor. He must have a huge brain ticking over inside that fluffy head of his. He would probably be a better leader than Louis, I think. He is, however, unhappy. It turns out his stepbrother Paul, who he hadn't seen for over one year, lost in a game of cricket catching with Louis and became a deserter. Paul then turned up as a pecan nut in one of Andrew Archdeacon's pies in Lower Mor's Den. Jim found the nut, tossed it to Max but he fumbled the catch. We then set off to find Paul. It was a bizarre start to our life underground, but Max has been inspirational in our challenges so far.

Eon has shown us his true nature; he was always a free thinking mouse. When I first met him in that prison many months ago he was like an older brother to me. He'd shield me from unwanted situations. He'd help me when feeding time came, so I didn't miss out, but when he became a free mouse, he changed. I like him, don't get me wrong, but like I've said before, his desires for revenge has always had control over him. He left us a few times in the early days of our escape. At first he was clumsy and became caught up in the cables hanging underneath the mechanical beast and ended up in Mor's Den. Then later, he ran off, first at Mor's Den and then at Cam's Den. And finally, at the lock, after being chased and cornered by some scratchers, he followed them. I think it takes a strong minded individual to follow your nemesis. I think we should let him go and allow him to sort his own life out. But what bugs me is that Louis wants us to find him even though Eon doesn't want to be found.

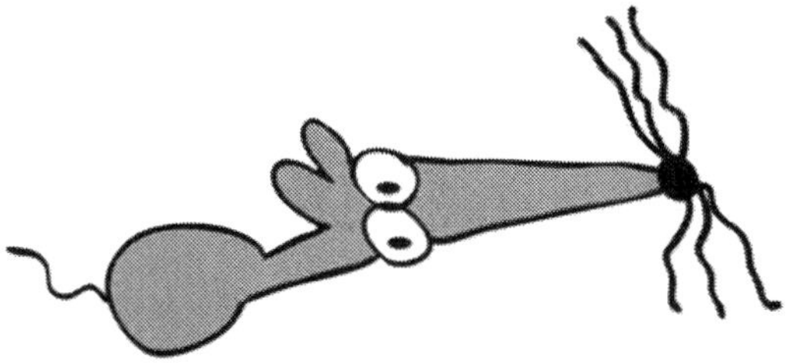

Jim is my favourite mouse. Yes, he is silly and has a fixation with his whiskers. Yes both his baseball-type hats and his clothes were ruined almost straight away; but he is cute. He is so proud of his appearance he makes me, the only female of our group, seem grubby. Alas he has a naïve attitude. Certain situations, when we really need solidarity, or when we need to listen or concentrate, he messes up. He has been the instigator of many of our problems. But weirdly, he has also been a contributing factor in how some of these expeditions have been solved. His luck, his dreams, his selfishness have provided a solution to many answers and puzzling riddles. His version of events can be somewhat exaggerated but his heart is in the right place. He is Eon's best friend and even he knows that Louis must let Eon go. He doesn't believe in the Scared Scrolls and he hates hamsters almost as much as he hates scratchers. He is always complaining and doesn't believe Louis is a very good leader at all.

The Ssssylfia is a strange manifestation that appears when the mechanical beast rushes away into the blackness. Louis believes it is an accumulation of our thoughts and wishes. Jim thinks it is smoke. I don't know what it is, but what I do know is that the Ssssylfia is helping us along the way. Without her guidance we would not have a clue where we were going. She is like a sixth sense. She is the difference between four confused mice with no direction in life, and four mice with a reason and a purpose. Ssssylfia has told us that Dark Energy is all around, yet not around. She has sets us riddles similar to the Sacred Scrolls and it begs the question: was this Ssssylfia around when the legendary Jerbil MacTaggart wrote the Sacred Scrolls 75 years ago? It is a definite maybe. What if the Ssssylfia is the presence of this legend? What if the legend is still alive? There are so many questions and so many answers that could be right. I wonder if I will ever understand the true meaning of Dark Energy. I wonder if this escape from our sawdust prison was a mistake. And I wonder if my life will end before it has begun…

Louis says we must mature to understand Dark Energy. But the *ONE* is the real reason why we exist. To understand all that lies ahead of us, to realise our potential in life and enjoy life, is our biggest goal. Yet the *ONE* is a puzzle that has no boundaries or limitations. What is this *ONE* and why is it so important?

As Volume Two begins new questions come to light.

If we are young and free, why do we need a leader?

If we all want to do our own thing and believe in our own dreams,

why do we have to comply with Louis' way of thinking?

Pour away your emotion and hunt in this wood,
for it is the things we do today
that will be remembered that are good

1. A Wild Goose Chase

In a time when freedom seemed the right way, a solution to all our dreams, I was confused. Louis again thinks Eon needs rescuing. But I don't understand why Louis can't see that maybe he doesn't want to be…

Our mission has changed. Well, we never had a mission before. We just wanted to be free and able to live our own lives. But now we have a purpose. It was tricky to find a world that we did not know existed and to realise that all our dreams and all our visions had been twisted.

"Friends, this morning we need to find Eon. But more than that, we need to find the lair of these evil scratchers for they hold Eon in their power," chanted Louis. "Eon wants to fight these scratchers and therefore he's bound to be drawn into their traps."

Louis stood, paws raised above his head as usual and he was smiling. He was so happy, so adamant that he was in charge that we'd have to listen. I hated him in his present state. He always used to care about me, but those days were gone.

We stood together on the higher level at Cam's Den and collectively felt sad. Then suddenly, out of the blackness the Ssssylfia appeared. It shimmered above Jim's head but as he tried to grab it, it faded away. Louis looked distraught. He closed his eyes and concentrated hard and, low and behold, the Ssssylfia appeared again.

"See Jim, no sooner have I spoken than the ghost mentions Eon again. I think we have to find him," grinned Louis. He was focussing hard on our faces, but he could tell we weren't happy about his suggestion.

"It's all very well you saying that we need to find and save Eon from these evil scratchers but we didn't complete anything yesterday did we?" reported Jim. "All we managed to do yesterday was discover lots of nasty things that lurk in our new world, or should I say, in your new world. Oops! I forgot we were going to call it Louis' World for a minute there, and as I forgot, what are you to do? Will you banish me to the end-of-the-tracks? Oh wait, I've been there already haven't I! Look, Louis, friend, comrade, let's skip Eon shall we. We hunted for him before, he obviously wants to live his life by his own terms, we'd be foolish, actually, we'd be down right unfair if we tried to tell him how to live his life. He's my best friend and I know it's time to let go."

Jim was unhappy. He was curled into a ball on the ground. He at first tried to wipe himself down with his tears. Then grasped his whiskers and dragged the dirt with his finger tips in an attempt to clean them. He hated being dirty and Louis' plans to go on another wild goose chase doubled his frustrations. The Professor was different. He seemed relatively happy. He had found his stepbrother, although Paul was still trapped inside the oversized pecan shell. Trapped in a similar way to the rest of us I guess. I don't understand why he doesn't try to open the shell with a pair of Max-Nutcrackers, surely that would reunite them.

Louis became impatient with Jim. "You just don't understand anything! Eon is a weak, stupid mouse. He needs the likes of me, the likes of the Professor to get him through this world. Not until I am convinced that he is ready will I permit him to stay where he wants."

"That means you want to be his parole officer. Hold his paw until he understands what lies ahead of him."

"Yes if you like, that's exactly it."

Jim was having a major argument with Louis on the meaning of life. Jim's argument was that Eon should live the way he wanted and make his own mistakes. Whilst Louis thought it was better to keep Eon in view, watch over him until he thought he was ready to face the world on his own. I have to say that for the first time in my life I'd sided with Jim, although strong arguments did hold Louis in good stead.

"What do you think Professor, should we ignore Jim's ideas or ignore Louis'?" I asked.

"Jane, I think we should get on with the matter in hand. We wouldn't feel happy unless we knew Eon was okay, correct? Therefore it's pointless arguing about his life now, when we're not really sure if he is even alive. What I think is that we should head for High Gate, only then will we be able to judge whether we are the right mice to preach the way of life to others. I feel that until we know everything about ourselves we are not in a position to dictate the law."

"I agree," I replied. "Let's quickly catch that mechanical beast to High Gate."

Jim seemed upset at the plan and wasn't really his normal, vibrant self. I do believe he hadn't really got too much sleep last night. Something was definitely troubling him. I watched as the others jumped on and I was about to join them when Jim attracted my attention. "Well I'm not going that way with them, come on Jane let's go this way. Let's look for this Dark Energy on a different track. Let's ignore them like they've been ignoring us all our short lives."

"No Jim, I don't want to go with you. I'll be much safer with the others don't you see? To be safe is much more important to me than just trying to prove a point. It is written that to break alliance with your team could result in fatal circumstances. I don't want to risk my life because of you. My life and my ambitions are what is important and if you can't understand that then I pity you."

"Pity me! Pity me! You fool. You're all fools. Can't you see what's happening? Are you all blind or something? It's Louis, he's brainwashed you. Don't be fool and come with me, Jane you must join me."

"I'm not playing a game with you Jim, this is real life! I just wish you'd step a little closer too, I hate shouting across a crowded higher level. Come on Jim, just look at those unpredictables over there," I pointed to about ten of them, "they're all watching us, and I kind of think this is all getting rather tedious."

"Tedious! Ha! You fool!" And with that Jim scurried off towards the other higher level alone.

I joined the others on the bumper of the mechanical beast and felt sad. I was ready to search for Eon but confused that Jim again snubbed our mission. Louis stroked my head and the Professor comforted me in my moment of need…

2. Jim's Dark Energy Expedition

And that was that. I couldn't believe Jim had deserted us, but worse, we were off to find Eon who probably didn't want to be found. I looked at Max and he seemed complacent but I could definitely see that without Jim, the trip may well be a complete waste of time. We stood there on the bumper still waiting for the mechanical beast to start up and pull away; it was a long wait.

"I though Jim was meant to be Eon's best friend," I squeaked. "Why has he just left us? Unless he knows something we don't."

"Search me Jane," answered the Professor. "Why do you think Jim's gone all odd Louis?"

"I believe he thinks he's becoming more grown up. Do you notice how he wants to single-handedly go in search of the Dark Energy. I feel for him. I'm sure he doesn't know what Dark Energy is."

"I reckon he doesn't know either although he told me what he thinks it is but it didn't seem a very good answer," I said. "Do you know what it is Louis?"

"Well, its location hasn't entered my thoughts at the moment, as I told you all on the day we escaped. The Ssssylfia spoke that it was in front of us yet all around us. Jim is a fool to rush off looking for something that he doesn't understand or even know what it looks like. My mistake was not leaving Jim in that jail all those days ago. In the sawdust prison he was happy. He was well fed, a bit too much really. He is not ready to explore as he cannot look after himself and now that he has run off, he may die. You see if we find Dark Energy or Jim finds it and we're not ready, then we'd waste our chance. We'd struggle to understand its meaning and sink into a state of low morale. And you all know what that can lead too, don't you?"

"No, what?" I asked and he still hadn't answered my question properly.

"Our brains would cease up. Our thoughts would turn to mush. We would lack drive. We'd no longer get excited by anything. We'd settle for what we have and we don't want to settle for what we've got now because we haven't really got anything, except ourselves. Did you get all that?"

"Well, sort of, but you still haven't said what this Dark Energy is?"

"Jane, please be patient. Things in my life have never been easy and I'm sure that understanding Dark Energy won't be either."

Suddenly the mechanical beast sprang to life and chugged off into the blackness. I thought it was strange that we kept getting these beasts to move around in. Louis always told us the Rat-Routes are the best way to navigate but it seems these Rat-

Routes are identical to the unpredictable's routes. I kept having this niggling question enter my thoughts; why aren't these Rat-Routes intergalactic pathways? That's what the Sacred Scrolls say, yet when we travel from place to place it's slow and noisy, bumpy and hot; oh yes, it's very hot. Yet at Cam's Den we did experience an amazing pathway so maybe these conventional routes that Louis makes us take are a mistake and not Rat-Routes at all.

"So what you're saying is you don't know what Dark Energy is then," I said to Louis. "Because Jim told me that it was the home of the notorious mouse-eating spider that lived in a town called Bell-Sized Park. The reason the spider chose to live in this park is that there's an enormous bell the same size as him that he rings when one of his servants delivers a prime, young, tubby mouse, ready for consumption. Jim told me that the Dark Energy is some kind of force-field wall that blocks all routes of escape. He said he had read in the Sacred Scrolls that crocodiles and alligators roam this park and can chew holes in this force-field. I didn't know whether to believe him or not. I know he does make stories up, that he exaggerates the truth sometimes, but it may be right. If we believe these Sacred Scrolls and we believe in all of them, then maybe Jim will solve this riddle before we do."

"But no, no, that's not right at all!" shouted Louis, "That spider will eat him for sure. Oh how can Jim be so stupid? I always thought Eon was stupid not Jim. All right Jim had an attitude problem but that was all. We've got to go to Bell-Sized Park straight away."

"But what about Eon? Which one are we to help? Why should we help Jim? Why not Eon?" moaned the Professor.

"Oh! Oh! We'll have to toss a coin for it. If it's heads we'll hunt for Jim and if its tails we'll hunt for Eon......here goes...."

The coin flew high into the air. It was a magical feeling seeing it up there and the funny thing was that which ever way it would land we would have to obey its command.

“So Louis, are you going to catch it or let it fall on the ground?” Max asked. He was wearing one of his Max-Gloves and seemed to be perched and ready to catch it.

“Professor, surely you know the answer to that. It is written that luck comes to those who wait. Now, who's luckier, Jim or Eon?”

“Jim I guess. But are you to catch it?”

"No, I must let it strike the surface in front of us. I must give it total control in our choice and destiny."

"That's very deep for you Louis. Deep and, well, almost fantastic. But not totally fantastic, as that sort of thing doesn't happen. Having said that it's been quite a complicated day so who knows....." Max smiled. He removed his Max-Glove and sat on the edge of the beast anticipating the result.

"Here it comes now..." I screamed. "It seems to be covered in dirt. You must have flicked it so hard and high into the ceiling that fragments of muck have spread themselves over the surface...... I think I can catch it...... shall I?"

"No Jane! No! Let it drop...." The coin came thundering down in front of us and became wedged between the bumper and the rear end of the beast in neither a heads or tails position.

"So Louis, now what?" Max asked. He was staring at the lodged coin and touching the jammed edges with his fingers. It was wedged in really hard.

"I guess, Professor, I'd better do it again." A second coin was thrust into the air. This one too jammed right next to the other coin.

"Louis, I think I should flick it," I suggested.

"You, why you?"

"Well I can't do any worse than you can I? Anyway, is it not written that it's the third time that's lucky."

"Well yes, but that means we can't flick it at all as you well know, because Jim's lucky," sighed Louis.

"So what are you suggesting?" I asked.

"I'm suggesting that we skip Eon and go back and find Jim," he replied. "I don't want to in my heart but, well, he's important to us all; you see he may have funny ideas but he has the gift of luck. Now, we all know that to defeat these scratchers in High Gate we need all the luck we can get. Let's jump off at the next higher level and head back."

As the mechanical beast chugged towards Arch Way, the Professor attempted to free the coins from the bumper. Then bizarrely, as this beast juddered to a halt, these coins just to popped out of their wedged positions and landed on the higher level in front of us.

"Look both coins have landed with their heads facing up. If one coin would not have been enough, both being heads is surely a sign from somewhere," I screamed.

"I knew that Jim was lucky. It is written that be you a mouse or hamster, two heads are better than one. Come on, there's no time to lose, that other beast is on the other side waiting for us, we can head back straight away," smiled Louis.

We all scurried over towards it, but, as we did so, out of the corner of my eye, I thought I saw Jim.

"Come on Jane, if you don't run now we'll all miss it," squeaked Max.

"But! But..." I mumbled.

"Jump will you!" Louis reached out and grabbed my right paw and pulled me on. The beast started up again and chugged once more into the blackness.

"Sorry," I mumbled, "it's just…"

"You were very slow then Jane, what's the problem?"

"Oh I thought I saw, well, it couldn't have been, but… I thought I saw… Jim."

"WHAT!" Max and Louis shouted simultaneously.

"Yeah! Ha! Ha! Jim."

"So why didn't you say? Quickly, we'll have to risk injury and jump off here," squawked the Professor.

"No Max!" But it was too late. The Professor had jumped off the moving beast and he bounced along the ground like a fluffy ball. Louis and I felt sad. Was our friend dead?

3. The Professor's Injury

"He'll be okay… I think," I mumbled. I stroked Louis' fluffy cheek. He had tears making their way to his chin so I gently wiped them away. Then we noticed the mechanical beast pull into the next higher level area, this being Cam's Den again. We both jumped off and ran to the other side to get the beast back to Arch Way.

"He's dead… he must be… I haven't in my life witnessed at such close range the death of one of my best friends…" Louis broke down into tears. I'd never seen him like this before; well actually I had once, but this seemed worse somehow.

"It'll be all right, you'll see," I answered as I tried to comfort him. I suppose this brought out the real mouse in him. I had started to believe he was crazy, like Jim had said. Like he was truly bonkers. Like he was a barmy machine on a mission that would let nothing stand in his way. Yet the loss, or potential loss, of a friend showed his weakness to me. Gosh, he must have thought I was quite strong to be unaffected. Maybe I was becoming stronger. Maybe the strength he has shown when we first left that prison was beginning to rub off on us. Hence the reason Eon went off to fight the scratchers and indeed why Jim had gone in search of the Dark Energy alone. Yes, certain things that I'm doing are starting to make sense.

"Look! Louis look!" I squeaked. As the beast came out of the blackness it arrived again at Arch Way. I didn't understand why this place had this name. I'm sure when Louis is in better form he'll tell us his version.

"Hang on… is that?" Louis became all agitated. He said, "Yes, look, it's Jim and the Professor. But look at the Professor he's all in a ball. He looks… No! No! He look's dead."

"Hi ya guys," grinned Jim. He seemed very happy to see us. He didn't realise the complexity of the problem, or did he?

"Why did you come back?" I asked.

"Well, I could tell a porky pie and say I missed you all, but that's not it at all. I wanted to help you find my friend, my good friend Eon. When I arrived in Bell-Sized Park I asked myself, do I really want to face a mouse-eating spider, battle against giant crocodiles and humongous alligators all on my own. I found the Dark Energy wall but I couldn't climb over it. I spoke to the spider; she's a bit weird. And something else happened, now what was that? Anyway, this odd spider said my reflection in this wall showed me as an unpredictable. I mean, how weird is that? She said that in a future life I'll assist round faces to explore. Fancy helping round faces! They usually hunt us and eat us so I thought, this spider must be mad. Well I wasn't gonna hang around there much longer I can tell you! I wanted to know that my best friend Eon was happy and safe, so I came back." He leaned his body against the ball of fluff that was the Professor and stroked him. Alas there were no signs of life.

"Crocodiles?" snapped Louis. "Are you exaggerating the story again? I don't care about you! Enough about you! The Professor has died because of you! I want nothing more to do with you!" Louis pushed Jim over in his rage. He blamed Jim for the Professor's death, that is, until we heard faint muttering noises.

"Urrr! I'm alive…"

"Who said that?" asked a confused Louis.

"I believe it's coming from the ball of fluff. I mean Max. Ha! Ha!" squawked a jubilant Jim.

"What, you mean he's alive?"

"I am," mumbled the Professor.

Jim scampered over to the Professor and tugged at his fur. "Umm! There seems to be a kind of strange netting around him, has anyone got any clippers? What we need is something short and sharp, well, do I have any offers?"

"This is not an auction. You can't dictate the run of play...." moaned Louis.

"Umm! Can you roll me please Louis? We need to find Eon before it's too late," groaned Max. He was awake but very tangled up.

"Yeah! I'll do that, you can count on me." Louis rolled the Professor along like a ball. We all clambered on the bumper of the beast and eventually headed for High Gate again. We had to tie the Professor on with his whiskers just in case he rolled off, which didn't look too comfortable it has to be said.

"If any of you lot ever tied my whiskers like that they would never be the same again," moaned Jim as he lovingly stroked his own whiskers. "After this escapade I'm going to have to have mine seriously manicured. I'll need the sprouting bays that I'm designing thoroughly overhauled after the first week, just think how ghastly that will be?"

"Stop talking about yourself will you, we're here," Louis shouted. We all jumped off. We couldn't untie the Professor properly so we had to unscrew half of the bumper and carry that along too. It must have looked a bizarre sight to the unpredictables that were watching us. One of them stopped supping from his bottle and started rubbing his eyes. Still, unpredictables have always had nasty habits. You'd never get a mouse looking so menacing and yet so stupid. I guess I was lucky to be born a mouse.

4. High Gate

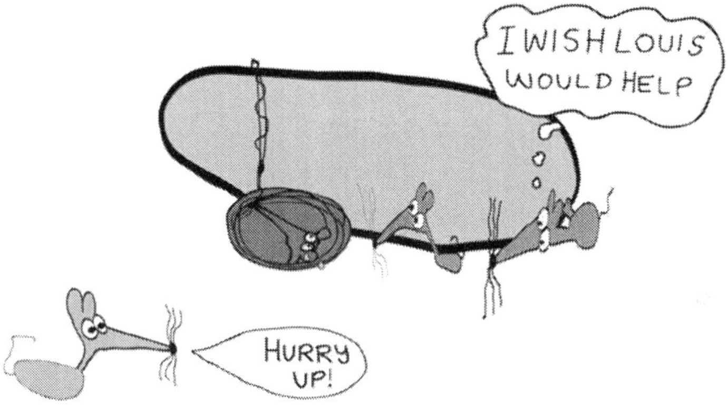

"Where are we off to now Louis?" Jim asked. He was very tired and moody, "and how come you're making me carry all the weight at the back of this bumper?"

"Will you stop moaning? Jane's watching the Professor and I'm trying to find this High Gate… there it is…" He pointed towards a large ginger mottled gate about two hundred yards in front of us.

"Wow! That looks high."

"Well Jim it would wouldn't it; that's why this place is called High Gate. If it was small I guess they would've called the place Small Gate," moaned Louis.

"I know! I know what you're trying to do, you're trying to rattle me. Well I'm not falling for it, understand!" Jim threw the bumper to the ground and one of the Professor's whiskers pinged off it, then blood began to pour from his fluffy face.

"Ow! Ow!" Max screamed. His cries echoed along the higher level and woke a dozing unpredictable. He looked at us mice and a tear formed in his eye. It was like he could understand Max's pain. Was this a sign that not all unpredictables were as dangerous as we thought? This unpredictable had greying whiskers and no earrings. He was slightly older than most that we'd seen. Louis then suggested that he probably sleeps on these higher levels too; so in a way he was just like us.

"Oh great!" moaned Louis. "So first of all you think I'm taking a pot shot at you and as a retaliation you hurt the poor, innocent Professor."

"It's not a game Louis, it's real life," I moaned.

"Will you all stop arguing and get me free from this bumper?" Max was even more miserable now his whiskers were broken. His grubby, dirty face was also blood stained. His glasses amazingly stayed on the whole time, but he was depressed. It must've been an awful experience for him.

"Yes Professor, all in good time," Louis replied.

Ahead of us there was what looked like hundreds upon hundreds of tiny cabbages. They were on the other side of the gate. Why were there cabbages here? I thought High Gate was known for scratchers not cabbages. It confused me, well, it confused all of us. The gate was itself on the other side of the tracks. We seemed to be walking down the tracks back towards Arch Way. So, was this cabbage kingdom really in High Gate or was it actually in Arch Way? Finally, we reached the base of a smaller gate. Although it had a lock on it, it was not the kind of lock we'd seen in Cam's Den. This lock was the type that fastens the gate's door or lid if it had one, which it didn't. We squeezed through the bars of this smaller gate and saw two rows of scratchers along the concrete lake. It was a horrible place.

“Look up there, on top of the really high gate,” cried Jim. “Isn't that… Eon?”

“Look how scared he is. And more to the point, look how high he is,” I said.

“What! What! What's going on? What's happening? Cabbages? Scratchers? I can’t see anything,” cried a troubled, spluttering Professor. He began wriggling so that he could see what all the fuss was about which caused him to slip from my grasp. I accidentally let go of him and although he seemed to be still fixed to the bumper, he rolled straight towards the gate.

CRASH!

“Oh no! Jane! What have you done!” screamed Louis. “How could you lose concentration like that? It is written that if you need anything, done properly, no matter how trivial, you're better off doing it yourself. Oh how foolish I've been. It must be due to the emotion that I feel inside. It's warping my judgement. But wait! Where's Eon gone now?”

“There he is… look!” I spotted him about fifty yards behind an army of green rats? They were in camouflage gear to make them, and I know this sounds silly, but, to make them look like little cabbages. Eon appeared to think he was running the show. He was the leader, the general. In the Sacred Scrolls it is written that *ONE* will come and save us all. Louis had the impression that he was the *ONE*, but maybe he wasn't, maybe it was Eon. Or maybe the *ONE* meant a team. That would be more realistic. Yes! A team of rodents would come and save our world, a team that would work in harmony to salvage a life for our children. Yes! Maybe Eon and his army of rat-cabbages along with Louis, the Professor, Jim and me, are this *ONE*, *the chosen ones*. We cannot let these scratchers win! That's why Eon had joined the rat army: because many hands make light work. It is not in our future to lose; I think not or at least I hope not.

"We'll have to leave the brave Professor here to take his chances," sighed Louis. "Jane, you'd better climb to the top of the gate. This was obviously a look out point for Eon."

I scampered off after receiving his instruction, but he carried on babbling as if I were still there.

"I reckon Eon was checking where his colleagues were Jane," continued Louis, "I never knew there were so many other rodents searching for Dark Energy. It is written that learning new truths about the world is the meaning of life. I never understood it before. I was always too naive. It's not until you see and learn about different cultures, different animals and how they survive that you can even start to understand yourself. I believe Eon will try to reason with these scratchers with assistance from the cabbages, I mean rats. There is no way Eon can defeat them alone. There are too many of them. They'll just keep coming back and back and back. I hope he's got a plan, I've never heard of a mouse that can negotiate a deal with a scratcher. True, he may become a weaker ally. That would probably have to be the first step. But I wonder whether his plan can guarantee safety forever. He'll have to pull the wool over the eyes of these scratchers in one way or the other. Maybe he'll contaminate the milk supply of our city and hold the export rights with other lands. Is he to negotiate a deal with these scratchers? Maybe we'll have to leave him here after this battle is over so he can fulfil his destiny. I wonder what *our* destinies will be. I wonder if we'll ever see Eon again after today. It is written that we should remember, remember, the eleventh cannon in a tower. What does that mean? What cannon? For alas I do not know what a cannon is. I wonder Jane, will I one day understand this Scroll?" He looked all around but I had gone. Jim was staring at him but seemed totally bored.

"Hey! Hey!" I was shouting at them from the top of the gate but Louis seemed to be in the middle of a flowing conversation and thus his hearing must have been switched off. All I could see was about ten scratchers dragging the Professor and the bumper off towards an arched chamber.

"Well?" asked a bored looking Jim.

"What?" replied Louis.

"You were going to say what we were going to do, and then you were off."

"Off? What do you mean, off?"

"You know, don't give me that. You were off on one of your fantasy trips. You were babbling on about Eon fulfilling his destiny or something. So what's our destiny? Oh yeah, and more to the point what's the Professors'? Because he's been dragged off by about ten scratchers over there," said Jim as he pointed. "I reckon his destiny is death, after all, you predicted that before didn't you?"

"What?" asked Louis. He was confused.

"The Professor's knocking on death's door," squeaked Jim. I watched as Louis swung his head from side to side in a desperate attempt to spot him.

"Quickly, there's no time to lose, we must rescue him, " I squeaked. But as I was high upon the gate and far away, my friends could not hear me, they snubbed me, sadness. Should I jump down and risk my life? Or should I stay safe high up here on this broken gate, far away from the dangerous and hungry scratchers that lurked down below. I was on the edge of reason. The Arch Way was enormous but the strength inside me grew. I wanted to see my friends again.

"Come on Jim, let's save Max," snapped Louis.

"But Louis we can't, look at all those scratchers, there's hundreds of them. We'd be dead for sure if we ran into their lair demanding sanctuary."

"That's it! You're right Jim! May I kiss the feet of the legend if I haven't got the dandiest of plans?"

"So? What are we to do?" asked a baffled Jim.

"We need Eon's help."

"Eon? Why can't we do it together, just me and you?"

"No! It's all about teamwork. Eon knows the rats that live here. They will know the scratcher's chamber inside-out. I believe Eon will want to deal with the chief scratcher on his own too. This town is becoming a fantastic place. Two of the biggest enemies living in the same area, yet they get along. If we need a negotiator it should be someone that will not lie and will do the job properly. Someone who will not talk nonsense of crocodiles or horrid alligators. We need an ally who can help us with nothing to gain except respect. Do you understand?"

Eon appeared, but Jim looked worried. Jim had spotted a scratcher behind Eon but his desperate attempts to warn him were pointless because the scratcher was friendly. Of course Jim didn't know this at the time and so he jumped the scratcher as Eon reached Louis. There was a terrible scrap. At one time I was sure that I saw Jim's tonsils in the scratcher's paw.

"Jim! Stop fighting! Are you okay?" Louis screamed. There was blood pouring from Jim's mouth, the scratcher had ripped his tonsils out but amazingly Jim seemed quite happy about it.

"Yeah, great. I've had problems with my tonsils all my life and not one silly vet would do anything about it. This is the happiest day of my life. It is written that if you own something that doesn't work and it has no value to you the best thing you can do is get rid of it."

"No it doesn't, you've made that up," squeaked Louis.

"Well, I think it should say that. Anyway, I sure scared that scratcher away. Eon! Hey, Eon, that scratcher followed you and I saved you. Come here my brother, my friend." Jim went over to hug his pal but Eon pushed him away.

"That was my only scratcher ally. I'll repeat, *ONLY* scratcher ally. You nearly cost all of us our lives."

"Sorry Eon, I didn't know," muttered Jim. "Well, no one ever said did they."

"No, I guess not," replied Eon. He went over to Jim and shook his paw. "In other words, I forgive you. Thanks for trying to saved me, my brother."

"I must remember not to try and save any other mice ever again," sulked Jim. He was in a relatively happy mood but still shocked by Eon's snappy manner.

"You can't mean that," groaned Louis. "All you have to do is think before you act or speak. It is written that if you open your mouth and say something stupid it's better that you say nothing at all."

"Umm," Jim mumbled. I climbed down from the gate and joined my friends. I explained that I had seen everything that had happened but was too far away for them to hear me. Louis seemed sad. It was his idea that I go to the top of the High Gate yet his plan had backfired. And now the Professor was probably heading for a scratcher's dinner plate while we were free. As we all headed for Eon's new home, deep amongst the underground woods, it was horrid to think about our captured friend's fate…

5. The Underground Wood

It was a cold night. The coldest we'd had for ages. I don't like the cold. When the mechanical beast is moving, when it is rushing through its tunnels it makes the whole place feel warm. But it had gone past its bedtime and therefore the underground wood was freezing. I looked at Jim and we both were puzzled. Why was the wood upside down? It was a strange place. Eon had only been here one day more than us but the story of his exploits was not that interesting, in fact I think I was the only mouse to stay awake for his tale. Jim on the other paw didn't sit with the rest of us. He loitered in the corner alone. He looked lost and confused. He was fiddling with his whiskers as usual but the more he tried to clean them, the dirtier they got. Both myself and Jim got up early the next day. Together we sat on the ground by the branches of the largest tree we could find and dreamt of our future.

"Jim you didn't listen to Eon's story last night did you?"

"No, was it interesting?"

"Yeah, do you want me to summarize it for you?"

"Go on then....." he replied.

"Right, after the trick you played on the scratchers in Cam's Den he decided there was no time like the present. He had to follow them as it seemed the right thing to do. Anyway the three scratchers had headed up a steep, winding concrete river along which were several unpredictables. Every unpredictable they passed would stroke them or give them food. But Eon had to hide in case any of the unpredictables informed the scratchers of his presence. He told me that he must have walked for miles. Tiny blisters started to grow on his hind paws. He said that he didn't like running on his front paws too much as it was difficult to manoeuvre. He said it made him feel like the legendary Jerbil MacTaggart. This Jerboa is a type of rodent that has stronger hind legs than mice and is good at jumping. He said that he came up to a large concrete island like the one in Mor's Den; but this one was much bigger. There was a vast building situated in the middle. And these scratchers seemed to enjoy risking their lives running across the concrete moat that seemed to flow around it. He assumed that these scratchers were chasing mice. Then he overheard that one legendary scratcher without claws was known not to eat mice. So it was fitting for Eon, to rescue this clawless scratcher from certain death."

"So you mean that the reason he's talking to that scratcher is because he saved it?" asked Jim.

"Yes that's it exactly."

"But how did he know that it wouldn't eat him?"

"I reckon it's because he reads the Sacred Scrolls quite often. He's got his own little book that he's written them all down in. He doesn't know as many as Louis or the Professor, but he knows more than me."

"So what about Max, does Eon know where the scratchers took him?"

"Yes, he said Max's life is in great danger as he has been put into a large cauldron. This pot is chained to floating platforms, but they are bolted down. He said these scratchers must use a magnet-type mechanism. Apparently Eon said that the rats were using similar magnets as flying machines. Weird eh? Eon says that the rats fly by allowing the same density pole magnets to react with each other. He said these strangely camouflaged rats are from the Rodent army. It's funny isn't it. I never knew there was a Rodent army and yet here we are with them. Well, maybe not totally with them, but they are on our side. Eon also said the scratchers in High Gate eat lots of mice and prefer them cooked. If we are to rescue the Professor we must be as cunning as they are. He said scratchers love to sleep and dream usually of dancing mice. He said this fact will aid our rescue mission."

"But I always thought that Eon was stupid, that he didn't care about the scrolls or what rats had to say. Wow! I'm really beginning to see him in a new light. When we were young we used to play in the prison and he would say silly things about a Rodent army but I just ignored him. Maybe he knew about these magnets and these rats and the Ssssylfia all along." Jim sighed and leaned his head towards me. "I like Eon, we are brothers but maybe this town is right for him."

"I think so too," I answered. We sat there and stared across at Eon and Grimley. Eon was snuggled in against the fluffy ginger scratcher and seemed happy. Grimley had his paw around Eon's body as though he was protecting him. It is written that black and white scratchers are the worst type. I thought this was a touch controversial. How can the colour of a scratcher determine how it acted. I knew this scroll was nonsense because back at Mor's Den the Professor was being given assistance by Colin (a black and white scratcher). He was on the side of the rats and helped in our getaway.

As we watched our friend Eon and Grimley sleeping Jim said he saw Louis out of the corner of his eye. "Look, Louis' running up to that cemetery at the end of the Higher Wood. Why do you think he's gone there?"

"Because he likes exploring," I replied. "But the problem with him going on his own to places is that if he's caught, or cornered by some scratchers, we'll never know. He should really stay with us. We are a team together, although sometimes I think he doesn't like being with us."

"Today's going to be a long day isn't it Jane? Louis told me that he believes Eon will stay here, with these rats and that scratcher Grimley. He says that Eon's destiny is with them. Quite interesting that isn't it? Eon being the first one to understand what he wants, what he needs to do. I often think of the day when I will know what I want to do. I think of what I may be doing this time next year, will it be fun? Or will I be doing the same type of thing. Will I always be wondering about stuff? What do you reckon? Do you believe the answer is staring me in the face and I can't see it? Do you believe that Dark Energy is the ability to wonder what is happening? Or imagining what could happen?"

"I don't know Jim, we're all different. That's the fun of it. Every mouse is an individual. We each have to make up our own minds where we're going. You must not let Louis control your every action as he wants to. He seems to me sometimes to be not quite there in the head. His ideas are a little over-the-top, you know what I mean, or not?"

"Yeah Jane, I know."

We must have been under that tree a while as we could see Louis scampering back down the hill towards us. I wondered what he had found. It was a funny hill. It was the first time in my life I've ever been to an underground hill, maybe it was to be the last…

6. Rescue Attempt

As Louis arrived he seemed worn out, but like always was trying to boss us around. "Hi there you two. What are you doing down here? It's time to go."

"Just talking, you know, thinking about things," replied Jim. He leaned right back against the trunk and placed his paws behind his head and for the first time in ages, he seemed relaxed…

"Well you'd better clear your brain of trivial things and join us as we search for the Professor," moaned Louis.

"I'll see you down there then," I replied. I stood up, stretched and headed down the slope.

"Good, see you in a minute," quipped Louis, "and are you coming Jim?"

"Depends… is that scratcher gonna be there?" Jim was sulking on the ground and looked upset.

"His name is Grimley. Don't just call him *that scratcher.* It is written in the...."

"Yes! Yes! I know what's written thank you very much."

"Jim, I'm impressed."

"Well, not all the Sacred Scrolls makes sense do they?"

"And what's that supposed to mean?"

"Oh nothing…" he muttered.

"Come on then, I'll race you down; last one has to kiss Grimley..."

"I'm not kissing that..." But Louis had already set off. "Oi! Well you could've counted to three and said ready, steady go! Come on! Come back!" Louis went flying passed my right shoulder almost knocking me over. He was really fast I'll give him that. Then about thirty seconds later, Jim came bumbling along cursing Louis... "Louis, cheating, not ready, cheating! Hi Jane... Byeeee!"

At the bottom of the hill was Eon. He didn't look very happy. "COME ON JANE WE'RE GOING NOW!" he bellowed. He was very loud. I'm sure he was showing off his good strong vocal chords. He sounded like a general as he bleated his instructions to his comrades. As it happens, only myself, Eon, Jim, Louis and that scratcher Grimley were going. The plan to rescue Max was complicated. Grimley was going to be our negotiator. Jim still didn't like the thought of a scratcher as a comrade but it was Eon's rules so, that was that. It was extreme of course. It was like an unpredictable having a gorilla playing go-between. Still, as we were meeting other gorillas, I mean scratchers, then so be it.

"Which way then Eon?" I asked.

"Right, we have to go past the second oak on the left, take a sharp right and then it's the fourteenth lair on the right. You can't miss it; there's a skeleton of a mouse displayed over the entrance."

"Charming," mumbled Jim

"What was that Jim, did you speak?"

"Nothing Eon, nothing."

"Come on let's go." Eon and Grimley led the way. Grimley towered above the rest of us, he was huge. It was really bizarre to have him as a colleague, but I didn't know if we were going to be just walking our way to one large dinner plate. Jim was paranoid about Grimley, he hates scratchers about as much as he hates hamsters.

"Eon, are you sure that scratcher won't just land us in deep water? Are you?"

"Trust, Jim. The answer to many things. That's the key. I trust you sometimes so why can't you trust me?"

"It's not you I worry about."

"What was that?" Eon moaned.

"Nothing..." mumbled Jim again. He stood between myself and Louis, he seemed happy next to two of his own kind. I suppose it was common sense really.

"It is written that trust and respect are not easily given, but can be easily lost," said Louis.

"I thought you were on my side," snapped Eon. "I don't need you encouraging him you know.... and another thing, that sack of the Professor's, where is it?"

"Err! I dunno?" Louis answered.

"I think he's got it with him," I muttered.

"Has he indeed. That's interesting."

"Eon, you have got a plan haven't you?" asked a worried looking Jim.

"How long have you known me?"

"All my life."

"Well then."

But I did see Jim's point because most of, or indeed all of Eon's plans in the past had been well, sketchy. He wasn't the most talented planner in the world. I guess he needed to unbolt the ideas inside himself. He was, after all, in High Gate to avenge his father's death. He was the son who needed to dismantle all his aggression to reach an understanding, a point to his life.

"So, and I'm not trying to be a pain but, well, what's this plan?" asked Jim. He looked very anxious.

"Grimley will distract the scratchers while we rescue the Professor, easy-peasy."

"So we'll just waltz in and waltz out with him, is that your plan?" moaned Jim.

"Well, two of us will. But we won't waltz we'll tango. It is written that it takes two to tango and I've picked you Jim as my dancing partner," smirked Eon.

"Are you crazy?" asked a shell-shocked Jim.

"I'd agree with that. Are you crazy?" quizzed Louis.

"Crazy? If only…" We all arrived at lair number fourteen. Grimley went to talk to the head scratcher. I was look out again. Jim and Eon would do the tango to distract the other scratchers and Louis would grab the Professor.

"I can't believe you really want us to tango," sighed Jim.

"Thinking about it, it's a game and you like games don't you?" grinned Louis. He was quite happy as he remembered the Dark Energy vision that the Ssssylfia had shown us. "It's that vision, do you remember?"

"Umm," he sighed. Louis was right this was that same vision. Jim laughed at me before because he assumed that I had been eaten or dragged away to my death, but now the egg was well and truly on his face. I was so glad that Eon had chosen me to be look out and not Jim.

"Don't get eaten," I said to Jim, grinning, but he looked distraught. He was terrified at dancing with clumsy old Eon, but worst, he would be tangoing in front of a group of hungry, nasty scratchers.

"Look, the scratchers are sleeping, if we dance while Louis frees the Professor the scratchers will just assume we are in their dreams. I know it sounds ridiculous but I've thought it through, it can't fail. The scratchers won't believe they're awake because it's so unbelievable."

"Your plan's unbelievable, and that's not a compliment," moaned Jim.

"Well, anyway, come on Jim, let's do it," ordered Eon.

The plan was set: Grimley had already gone, drawing lots of other scratchers away leaving a circle of ten guarding the Professor. The scratchers must've cut Max's whiskers because he was free from the bumper but, worse than that, he was in a large cauldron. I suppose the scratchers were making a kind of mouse stew. The Professor was no longer in a ball, he was swimming around in the pot. At one stage it looked like he had a radish poked in his mouth. He also seemed to be using the stalk of a leek to stay afloat. It seemed that Louis' rescue attempt wasn't going to be so clean cut.

Louis sneaked passed the first scratcher; it seemed to twitch its nose as he went by. It could obviously smell him. He scampered by the others before reaching the base of the cauldron. Eon and a terrified looking Jim took up their positions in front of the scratchers. Louis, using a stray noodle climbed to the top of the pot, but then disaster: as he reached the top he lost his footing, slipped and he went crashing to the ground into a bowl of onions. This woke up one of the scratchers. This scratcher fluttered its eyelids. Eon and Jim then started to dance the tango. Eon was playing the part of the female mouse and he'd brought along some maracas as props to click at the right times, thus simulating a real tango scene. The scratcher at first looked shocked. It then noticed the others sleeping, rubbed its eyes and settled back down to sleep. Louis emerged from the onions, I saw him pop his head out as I was right up by the horrible mouse skeleton display. It was a ghastly spot but I had the perfect view to warn them should any other scratchers come our way.

Anyway, the Professor had obviously seen Louis. He threw over another noodle once he saw the coast was clear. The Professor then tied his end of the noodle to the leek he was holding. Louis again climbed to the top of the cauldron. He reached out his front left paw, the stronger of his four paws, grasped the Professor by five of his whiskers and plucked him from the pot. His whiskers were very short and very springy. Two of them snapped clean off while he was being pulled out. Then they both fell into the onions again. The crash caused another scratcher to wake. Eon and Jim started their tango routine and the scratcher fell for it, dozing off again. Louis, the Professor, Jim and Eon then rushed towards me. We embraced and fled.

Eon said that Grimley would join us later but that now we had to get back to our hiding place. We arrived back quite quickly. Eon looked happy but tired; having said that, we all looked tired.

“I'm staying here with my new rat colleagues and Grimley. I’m going to try and make a go at living here. It's the most beautiful place I know. If I left I know I'd be making a big mistake. It is written that opportunities knock twice in a lifetime. My first was when we broke free from that prison, and the second is the chance for me to live here, for me to make it work for my new, adopted society. I believe I can do it. I understand I need to find the Dark Energy, but not until I've sustained a working knowledge of my friends and my thoughts will I even begin."

"It's sad for us to see you leave us friend but I'm sure we'll meet again." Louis shook the right paw of Eon. Jim smiled at Eon and seemed to just walk away. I kissed him on the left cheek and ran back to join with my friends. The Professor also just smiled. He was badly shaken up by the ordeal. His whiskers would never be the same again, but then again neither would his memories. We waved from the underground hillside and then disappeared back to the broken gates of High Gate to fulfil our own destinies...

"So what are we going to do now then Louis?" asked the Professor. He was sitting by the big oak tree and wiping the sweat and the stew juices from his brow. He then cleaned the smeary marks from his Max-Glasses before he slumped on the ground, exhausted.

"Well, we've still got to try and somehow turn Paul back into a mouse haven't we, we can't leave him as a pecan all his life."

"Oh, hang on! Err! Max! Ha! Ha! Actually this is not funny," mumbled Jim.

"What?" asked the Professor.

"Err! I think I dropped Paul in Bell-Sized Park when I was looking for the Dark Energy, sorry...."

"Jim, although you can tango relatively well you're most certainly not the most reliable," sighed Louis. Still I suppose in your own little way you've set up our next mission, to search for Paul again, if this pecan is Paul that is…"

When there is no movement and emotions take command, the truth may hurt but answers will be found

1. Security Breach

We scampered past the broken gates, saw the Arch Way ahead and the thoughts of never seeing Eon again made us feel sad. But, our fruitless search to be reunited with our friend did have a purpose. For Eon had discovered part of his destiny. The question now was would he live to regret it. We arrived at the Arch Way's higher level but it was dark and cold. It wasn't night but something or someone had changed this world. I shivered; the hairs on my back stood on end. I was scared, well, we all were. I huddled next to Jim and as we tried to doze off together…

"I can see it now as the lies unfold, the time is three, it's cold; three in the morning that is. I reckon we're sleeping here tonight and starting afresh in the morning," groaned Louis. He was shivering too and looked worried. I was sure he was waiting for the Ssssylfia to arrive and assist us with our next task. But the Ssssylfia doesn't tend to come for us unless the mechanical beast arrives. He looked distraught. He said it was three in the morning but I was sure that it was later than that. What worried me the most was why the higher level was so cold? Where was the beast? What was happening?

"But it is morning Louis and it's not three it's eight thirty in the morning," answered Max. He too was shivering.

"Professor, if it was eight thirty it wouldn't be this cold down here would it? If it was eight thirty the place would be teaming with lots of loud, argumentative unpredictables, all of whom would be pushing and shoving. At eight thirty in the morning it's boiling in here. It's probably its warmest time, and I'm freezing."

"But my Max-Clock says eight thirty."

"Well maybe you broke it, after all it has been a rather hectic week."

"No way! It's shockproof this. You could fall off High Gate and die and this Max-Clock would be working as well as day one!"

"I'm just not getting through to you am I. Look all around. It's dark, yes. There's not a single unpredictable in sight. There's no warm beast at all. It's so cold it feels like the middle of the night, do you understand?" Louis was strutting about. He was waving his hands in the air and cursing Max's name. It was cold, but there was no need to be so rude.

"It is odd, I agree."

"It's not odd for the early morning," moaned Louis. "Look down there, both Jane and Jim are trying to sleep. They don't sleep during the day usually do they? Well do they?"

"I wouldn't say we know what a usual day is anymore!"

"Look, what more proof do you need. If you want we can scamper up the escalator and see the black of night outside, is that what would make you happy?" moaned Louis.

"Yeah, I'm sure it'll be daylight," answered Max. He was becoming grumpy and Louis just didn't believe a word he said. The arguing meant that my attempted sleep was just that, attempted without being successful.

"Hey, what's all the noise about?" I moaned.

"Oh sorry to wake you Jane, but the Professor seems to think it's in the middle of the unpredictables' rush hour."

"But it's freezing and there's no one about, how can it be?"

"Exactly. Come on then Professor let me prove you wrong." I watched them scamper along the higher level towards the escalators, but the silver steps weren't moving like before, it was as though the whole area had become a morgue, a place which only the dead haunted. Surely this was a sign that told the Professor that it was the middle of the night. What was wrong with him?

"Look, all these steps are killing my back, do you still not believe me?" growled Louis. We'd had a torrid time trying to rescue Eon and now we all wanted to do was rest but the Professor wasn't helping by making us prove him wrong.

"Well Louis, why should I believe you if you don't believe me? It is written that seeing is believing. Now we'll see who's right and who's wrong."

I decided to get up and go with them. I felt sad to leave Jim all alone but foolishly I forgot to say that I was coming.

CRUNCH!

"Ow! You trod on me!" I screamed.

"Hi Jane, I didn't see you down there, sorry," sighed Louis.

"I thought I'd tag along too, as you woke me up." We scrambled up the steps and were blinded by strong sunshine.

There were railings across the entrance of the station. Outside there were hundreds of unpredictables waiting for big, red machines. It was odd. I remember asking Louis to pinch me as I'd never seen anything like it. What was happening?

"See, I told you it was eight thirty in the morning. Actually it's eight thirty-five now. It is odd though. I wonder why these unpredictables have closed the building down. Maybe a scratcher is loose on the line. Maybe Jim's being eaten as we speak. I think we'd better go back down and wake him. I believe we're a safer unit if we are all together rather than split up."

"Yeah! I agree. I should've believed you but it's odd this, very odd." Louis looked stunned.

He was gazing through the railings thinking to himself, in his own little world. Having said that there was nothing else we could do except think. We had to somehow solve this riddle. The ironic thing was that the Ssssylfia usually supplies Louis with the riddle so maybe this time the ghost would supply the answer, if indeed we saw her. The Ssssylfia seemed to live inside the beasts, so if there were no beasts maybe there would be no Ssssylfia…

2. Stuck in Limbo

"Come on, let's go down and join Jim," shouted Louis and we followed him back down the steps. Jim was still lying in the same position as we'd left him, which was a relief. The Professor's thoughts of a scratcher on the line were fortunately, untrue.

"So what do we do now then?" asked the Professor. "We can't walk to this Bell-Sized Park place can we. Well, we can, but we don't know which way to go and it's probably miles and miles away. My stepbrother Paul will think we've left him again. This isn't going be good for him you know. He was always such a confused mouse. I remember once when we were runts together, all our other brothers and sisters were grown bigger than us and they used to bully us. We were friends forever. If either of us got into any scraps the other would be on hand to help. You see, brotherly love was important. I remember once, a real long time ago, long before the revolution that would change our forefathers' thoughts. It was a..."

"Did you really have four fathers?" I asked.

"No, I don't think so! Our forefathers were the eyes of our past. It's one of those words that Louis likes. It has a couple of meanings. But as he told you before it's the way the sentence is worded which determines how the answer is conceived. Do you get it?"

"No not really. But please continue anyway..." We all sat with our hind paws dangling over the edge of the higher level. Jim woke up and yawned. He looked towards me with dopey eyes and snuggled against me. Louis decided to lie on the higher level behind us and then spun round onto his tummy. He said he was listening with his eyes closed, but neither myself, Jim or the Professor believed him.

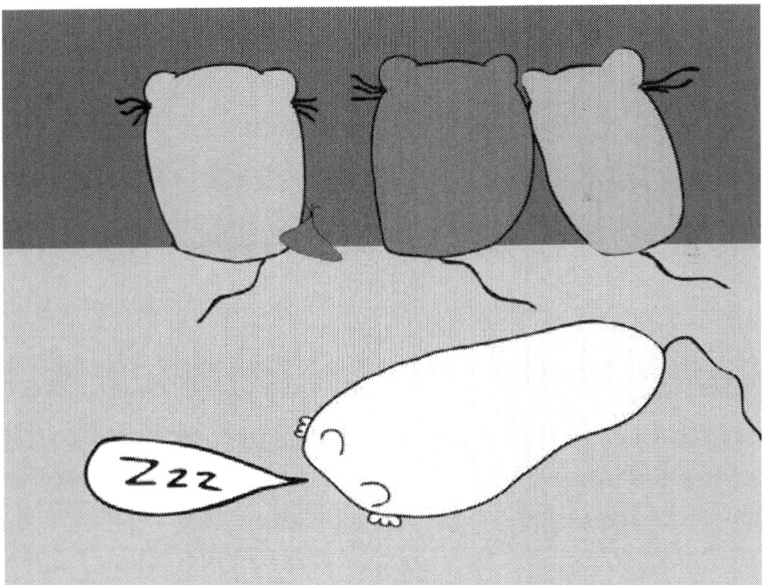

"So, anyway Jane, the revolution occurred one stormy night on board a luxury cruise liner on its way to the other country. That's how many of our cousins made it across the Great Sea. Anyway, heading the revolution was a small rodent with big ideas. The fact that he was born a runt and struggled throughout his life to be recognised as more than a common-or-garden rodent was important. Louis is always saying that if you prove yourself to yourself then you'll be content in yourself. Right where was I? Oh yeah. This runt, this tiny, weenie, little guy was nicknamed Pigmy Broth by the scratchers where he grew up. He used to dress himself elegantly. Jim would've been proud to know him, I think. As time tottered onwards he became fascinated by the colour crimson. He'd wear crimson shoes, a crimson cloak, but his trademark became a crimson scarf that he wore round his little fluffy neck come rain or shine. His nick-name Pigmy Broth, was soon to be changed: he'd become Crimson Pigs. It is written that a rodent wearing a crimson scarf could light up the air just by chanting a laugh. Yes, he was a happy-go-lucky rodent. I've often wondered if we'll ever meet him. Oh, I seem to have gone off the point a tad, hang on.... Right, Crimson Pigs was the ring leader in the stowaway ocean-crossing saga. You see it made him feel big. Big, the one thing he was not. He used to manage to get at least four mice in each suitcase that went abroad. He alone knows how he managed to do it. He was an inventor like me. I often wondered what kind of device could conceal four mice inside locked suitcases. I thought that maybe it was a lie. I know this sounds a little terrifying but he must have done something odd. I thought that maybe he got paid his ration of peanuts from the fools that would succumb to his trap, then he'd dispose of the bodies. Well, no mouse that I know has ever gone to the other country and come back to tell their tale, so who knows? A slightly more obvious way of doing it would be to have invented an invisible cloak or sack. He was, after all, a clever rodent. I think he was a crossbreed, just like the legendary Jerbil MacTaggart. If I, with inferior brain power, can think of ways to make my inventions and store them as tablets the list of possibilities must really be endless. I wonder if size is important. For I am a small mouse and seem to display certain (and I don't mean to be too modest) talents. It is written that size isn't important. But I've never met any tall or indeed normal sized rodents that can dictate to the world in the same way as Crimson, myself, or indeed my friend and stepbrother Paul."

"Paul the pecan. Ha! Ha!" joked Jim. The Professor's endless babbling had disturbed Jim and woken him up.

"It's not funny that Paul's a pecan you know."

"Professor, yes it is. Why don't you try laughing, you may get a shock, you might like it. Ha! Ha! It is written in the Sacred Scrolls of Jerboa that if you don't have a laugh now and then there's something wrong with you."

"It doesn't say that," moaned the Professor.

"All right, it doesn't, but maybe it should."

"Did you listen to my story Jim?"

"Story?"

"Yes story."

"What?"

"What do you mean, what?"

"Eh?"

"Hello! Hello! Calling planet Jim, are you receiving me?"

"Are you all right Professor?"

"I am. I can't say the same about you?"

"What?"

"There you go again."

"Eh?"

"Will you two stop!" I screamed at the top of my lungs.

"Stop what?" giggled Jim.

"I can't take it any more...." replied the Professor. He then dipped his hand into his sack and pulled out two inventions.

"What are they?" asked a baffled Jim.

"I don't know why I'm talking to you but this invention here's called Max-Mirrors. You see how they all sit at different angles. Well, I can place them from here all the way up the escalator to the exit. Therefore we can tell if the unpredictables have opened the railings."

"Eh? Don't waste those mirrors, I can use them to see my whiskers and maybe unclog them."

"Don't start that again Jim. And the other invention's called Max-Plugs. I can pop them into my ears and then I can sit in peace and not listen to your childish arguments or I can sleep like Louis has behind you. Ha! Ha!" We turned and saw Louis asleep just like the Professor had said and then watched as he rushed off alone towards the escalator with his Max-Mirror invention. Myself and Jim just stared at him. Oh how bored we were…

3. The Truth Comes Out

"Jane, why's the Professor gone off with those mirrors, I didn't understand?"

"For some reason the station is closed. Louis says we have to stay here and be patient. The unpredictables are unreliable you see. They can't run an efficient service. Everything's got to be complicated. Louis said before we go to Bell-Sized Park we should try to understand the Ssssylfia's riddle. But we can't do that if there is no beast, because without this beast there will be no ghost and therefore no riddle."

"So what are we supposed to do in the meantime, just wait. Just stare aimlessly at the walls, daydream our lives away, is that it?"

"Yep, that's about the size of it." The Professor had gone off to fulfil his plan. Louis had dozed off, which just left me and Jim chatting.

"Bored! Bored! Bored!" Jim was running up and down the higher level, each time timing himself on the Max-Clock that the Professor had left behind. But the more he ran, the more tired he got. Eventually he came right up to me. He was dripping with sweat, and exhausted. "It is written in the Sacred Scrolls of Jerboa that when you're bored out of your mind you should exercise, then if you die at least you died whilst you were doing something."

"Jim, it doesn't say that."

"Well it should! So Jane, do you know any stories that you can feed me to ease this boredom that sings in front of us like a parade of laughing scratchers? Anything will do, honest. Well, anything that doesn't involve Louis. How about before you got to the prison? Or how about a tale of your family? Have you got any family left?"

"Family. Now there's a word I haven't heard for a long time. Yes I have got a family, although I think both my parents have passed away. Well they must have, as us mice don't live forever do we? Let me take you back in time Jim. To a time when we ran free. To a time when we used to watch the blossom float from the trees. To a time when we were happy and content. This was the time when we didn't understand what the world was like. We… I say we, because I was born into a family of all females. There were seven of us. Seven young female mice together. Oh how the good times of my youth seem to stay as vivid in my mind as if they were only yesterday. I loved being around my sisters. We lived in a community where there were no male mice. I do believe that without males to feed us lies we'd all be together today. I still think about my sisters at night. I wonder if I'll ever see their little fluffy faces again. I mean some of them could be dead and

I'd never know. We used to think we were put on this earth to have fun. I know you think I must have been out of mind to be so naïve, but we really did think that life was there to be enjoyed. It was not until we were split up from each other that I really realised what we'd had together. It's funny isn't it. You live your life taking things for granted then suddenly, BAM! Your whole world falls apart. There were so many things that I wanted to say to my friends and my sisters. Oh, just thinking about it makes me sad. It is written that to show emotions is the sign of a real mouse and that to hide them, to bottle them up, is the sign of a fool. Oh how foolish I must have been. I wonder if it was as plain as the nose on my face. After all, I probably had the biggest nose of all my sisters. In fact I think that my nose could be entered into the world record's book as…"

"Yes Jane, I think I get the picture. Look, why don't you give me a race to the other end of the higher level and back, that'll be something to do?"

"Okay then, after three. One… two… threeee!" We both scampered up to the far wall and back to where we started. Jim won.

"Now what?" he asked. He was soaked in sweat, and I have to admit so was I. We must have looked a scruffy pair. Jim was usually so tidy. He tried to comb his whiskers at least twice a day, but this morning was an odd morning as Jim had woken up last. I guess he was dreaming of his previous life with Eon, now that it was over. He looked so messy this morning it was amusing and the funniest thing was, he didn't care. Was living in the underground world changing him inside? I believe so. He couldn't even wear his spare baseball cap. I say spare because his favourite one blew off his head on the day we escaped and landed in a fish tank. He then lost his spare one when he became trapped under an unpredictable's shoe and now his hair is all over the place. The funny thing is he doesn't comb his furry head anymore. Gone are the days when he was clean and tidy. Yes, definitely from about the time we left Mor's Den he had become uncharacteristically scruffy.

"So where's the Professor gone again?" asked a bored looking Jim. He was attempting to do a headstand but every time he tried he fell flat on his furry face.

"You are silly! Anyway, Max said he was going put some mirrors out or something."

"Do you reckon we should go and look for him?"

"Yeah, maybe in a minute, let me just finish off my story."

"Oh sorry Jane, I thought you had."

"Right, us sisters, we joined a commune. It was a community run organisation where there were no males. Well, that's what we thought. In fact there was one male there, his name was Louise."

"But Louise is a female name isn't it?"

"Yes. It is written that with an educated guess nine times out of ten you'll hit the nail on the head."

"What nail?" asked Jim, confused.

"It's a figure of speech. We guessed that because this female called Louise had a deep, gravelly voice there was definitely something fishy going on."

"So?"

"So we investigated. We discovered that this mouse was from a long line of mice impersonating other mice. She came from a family of fourteen you see. This mouse was the second youngest member, called Louise the thirteenth. But there was a case that she was not what she seemed and was actually male! But there was so much inconclusive evidence it couldn't be proved. I guess at least it brightened up an otherwise drab day."

"But I thought you said you liked the old days?"

"Well that's funny because my memories seem to get better the longer the time drags on. It's true I'm bored out of my mind talking to you on this higher level, but maybe in six months it might seem more interesting."

"If this waiting gets interesting can you tell me, I'd really like to know what I'm missing."

"Anyway back to this sneaky mouse Louise. So by her errors we discovered that *she* was actually a *he*. One day she was merrily scampering by an old mill on a hill. This was the place that we used to go and play when we were young. It was my heaven. Anyway, this Louise character was carrying some corn to the mill so she could crush it and make a corn soup and we managed to talk her into staying for supper. But the soup she made tasted nasty. It was as though she'd been brought up without the knowledge of corn cooking. Now everyone knows that all females are taught how to cook corn and yet she forgot one vital ingredient you see, the right paw sized scoop of salt."

"Is this important? Is it? It had better be soon otherwise I'm going to join Louis in dreamland."

"So, Louise told us the truth, that she was really a male mouse. She was upset at her deceit, or should it be *his* deceit? Anyway, Louise told us it wasn't *his* fault as *his* name was picked by *his* mother. Anyway after his admittance we forgave him. He then told us the most obvious trademark of a female named mouse that was actually male would be observing their sleeping position. Louise said a female mouse is closed off, whilst a male spreads his entire body length across the floor. This is a sign of territorial significance. I've watch you sleep Jim, you spread yourself, the Professor too. But looking at Louis makes me think that maybe he might have fallen under the mistaken youth trip and may have been brought up as a female. For if you place a letter *E* after his name does he not too become a *L-O-U-I-S-E…*"

My explanation to Jim about our leader probably being born and brought up as a female has unfortunately caused Louis some problems and at present, he is unaware of this. I like Louis, but he has been arrogant and nasty recently. I like Jim too but when you sit and chat to someone when you're bored sometimes too much information can cause problems.

"Hey yeah, I never noticed that before," squeaked Jim. "Louis is really Louise! He's been hiding that from us hasn't he? He must have been mistaken for a female at birth. Ha! Ha! But isn't that a bit dangerous for him? If other mice or indeed hamsters discover that our leader has a female name surely they will laugh at us? They will mock us. Oh the shame! Oh how could I have been so foolish as to let Louis get away with this insult. The swine! The cheater! It is written to never trust a mouse whose eyebrows join in the middle. I always knew Louis was nothing more than a cheat. He lied to us didn't he? Don't you know what that means? It means he doesn't care two hoots about us. Look at him lying there crouched with his stomach facing the ground. Oh the shame of it. Oh the shame!" Jim was fuming. He was stomping his feet and waving his arms in air. It all got a little too much for me, I have to admit.

"I don't think he did it to spite us. He's probably just embarrassed you know. Well wouldn't you be? If you were not called Jim and called say *J-I-M-A*, wouldn't you drop the *A* just to make you appear male, well?"

"Look I'm not the issue here! He's the cheater, the liar, not me! I'm going to wake him that's what I'll do. I'll soon sort him out. I'll let him know that I'm not scared of him anymore."

4. Jim's Frustration

"Stop Jim!!" I squeaked. But it was too late. Jim had found a half filled can of some nasty unpredictable drink and thrown it at Louis.

SPLOOSH!

The very smelly pineapple juice flew through the air and the juices soaked Louis. He woke up and started to complain. "What the? What are you up to Jim? Yuk!"

"So you're awake. Well why didn't you tell us eh? Why did you have to cover up the truth. It is written that truthful mice are friends but liars are enemies."

"Liars? What are you on about? What's rattled your cage this time? Yuk, I'm all sticky." Louis started to wipe the drink off himself but the more he rubbed at it, the dirtier he got; fluff from his paws stuck to his face and got in his mouth; he wasn't happy at all.

"Why did you tell us your name's Louis when really it's Louise? Well answer that one if you dare?"

"How did you know that? What's going on? So what if I changed my name. Any mouse can change their name but it is what's inside that counts."

"Argh! But is it not true that you were brought up as a female. You learnt to live your life as a second...?"

"I am not a second! I was born Louise, yes. But I am Louis now. I have always been a male mouse but learnt female ways as my mother named my older brother and me, Louise the thirteenth and fourteenth respectively. We two brothers were male mice and with this female name we understood female as well as male logic, this is why I may be the *ONE*! It won't be my brother, as he died."

Louis broken down in tears and I was moved by his explanation. However Jim's rude comments about females forced me to snap at him instead, "Hey that's a bit strong. Just because you think females are weak doesn't mean they are. Us females have a stronger hold on morality than males. Probably the thing that makes Louis stand out from the rest is that he's seen life from the female point of view. You see, ignorant mice like you Jim don't understand us females. We are the same species but we live our lives on a different wavelength. Louis, I would guess has adapted both worlds into one. Maybe he is the *ONE* that the Sacred Scrolls talk about. Or maybe it's our strength as a unit that is the key. If we all curse and tease and put each other down all the time we'll only get bitter. We must unite not argue.

"Rubbish," moaned Jim.

"It is written that it is unwise to bite off more than you can chew," I groaned. "I believe knowledge is the food of life with Louis, and without him you would have died of starvation a long time ago."

"Typically you're sticking up for him. Is it through faith or love I ask myself?"

"It is also written that there is a thin line between love and hate. But for me there is an enormous line and as each day ticks by that line gets wider?"

"Whatever!" screamed Jim as he scrambled towards the escalators, then he yelled, "I'm going to try and have a decent conversation with the Professor, unless of course I find out he's really called *M-A-X-I-N-E*!"

"Faith. Where's his faith Jane?"

"I don't know anymore. He gets one idea into his head and he starts ranting away."

Then Louis tried to explain himself to me again, he was panicking, I'd never seen him look so unhappy. "Look, I had to lie about my name as it's embarrassing. Maybe I should have told you all straight away, got it all out in the open. Still everyone knows now, well, except the Professor, but I'm sure Jim will tell him."

"Yeah, I mean things aren't going to get awkward for you because we know are they? You yourself said that it doesn't matter. So I'm sure as soon as we leave this higher level we'll forget about it."

"Yeah, well, try telling Jim that."

Both myself and Louis headed upstairs to see the others. When we got there we saw Jim gazing through the railings, he looking sad. I remember seeing a tear in his eye as he turned towards us. "Oh, hi, there's not much to say really except that we'll never see the Professor again."

"Jim, what do you mean?" I walked right up to him. He pointed to some hairs on the railings and then to some drops of blood. He knelt down and starting to cry. It was awful.

5. Was the Professor Snatched?

We all gazed out through the railing towards the concrete river and saw hundreds of unpredictables queuing for big red mechanical machines. I think these are called buses in the unpredictables' language.

"It looks like some nasty scratcher had him," cried Jim. "Oh the shame I feel. Oh how I should have been there for him in his moment of need. Why is this world so cruel? Why has it first taken Eon from me and now the Professor, why?" He broke down in tears again. His whole fluffy face became drenched. He just lay on the ground in front of us punching the floor with his right paw. The reason he used his right paw was because he was grasping something in his left, but he was lying on it so we couldn't tell what it was.

"What's that underneath your body?" I asked.

"What?" he groaned.

"That, there, what you're lying on."

"Oh it's the Professor's sack of inventions. That's how I know he's definitely gone forever, he'd never leave them behind would he?" He started rubbing his eyes but the more he rubbed the redder they got. It was as though he was allergic to his own fur.

"So do you think we should try and find him then Louis?" I asked. As we gazed through the railings, we hoped he was safe and still alive, but we didn't know for sure.

"To be honest with you I'm not sure Jane," sighed Louis. "You know what the Professor's like, once he's got an idea in his fluffy head he takes the initiative. He does what he feels he should do, but for me it's different. I feel that we should stay here. We don't know which way he's gone do we? It is written that the law of averages says stay put when the roads lead to nowhere special. If we saw a sign indicating a grassy common in half a mile on the right, then it would be pretty obvious where he's gone. But as there's no sign I believe that to stay here is our best option."

"So leave him to die alone, is that it? Let the blood pour from his gaping wounds and allow him to die around the next corner, great," growled Jim. "I always thought you didn't like the Professor. This day is becoming my day of reckoning, more so than the first. Louis you've got a nerve. Ha! I can't believe you're just going to leave him out there to face the dangers alone. Well I'm not. I'm going down to those chocolate machines on the higher level to steal some vital energy food. With his sack of inventions, I alone then, must find our comrade. Don't worry Louis, when I find him not only will I tell him of your cowardly games but also that you've got a girl's name. I bet he won't believe me; but will you lie to him and carry on with your deceit?"

"Go if you feel your destiny is to die in this place. Unfortunately mine is not," answered Louis. He looked stunned by the guts Jim had shown as he had always been such a coward. But now it looked like Louis was being the coward. I remember one of the Sacred Scrolls saying that it is possible to fight with the mind as well as the paws. I guess Louis was trying to keep in control of the situation. That's what made him our leader. But sometimes he did, I feel, make the wrong decisions…

6. Mutiny

We watched as Jim scampered off towards the escalator. He still had tears running down his face, but it was as though they gave him inner strength. It is written that when you need extra strength something inside your heart can open another door to it. Never before had I really understood some of these scrolls, but I was beginning to now. I followed Jim, for although he seemed in control of his actions it's at such times that a mouse can be more vulnerable. A confident mouse tends to make silly, almost obvious mistakes.

He was about ten steps ahead of me. I hid from him every time he looked round so he didn't think I was prying into his affairs. I remember turning back towards Louis just before I reached the stair that would put him out of sight and he looked sad. I guess in his eyes he thought I too was deserting him. He was always such a paranoid mouse. If you said or did anything vaguely to do with him he'd be on you like a ton of bricks. He'd be questioning you. I think that's what gives him the edge over the other mice that I've met: his never say die attitude. His willingness to handle danger. His faith in his ability to pull off the vital back-paw return to the furthest corner of the court from an impossible angle. Well, impossible to a normal mouse, but not to one who believes so heavily in himself.

I turned and looked again at Louis, he wasn't coming and I felt dejected, then I felt a different paw stroke my face. It was Jim. He still looked upset but at least he was happy to see me.

"Jane what are doing following me? Have you come to help?"

"Err, yeah. Look, let me give you a helping paw."

We scampered together along the higher level and both stood in front of an enormous chocolate machine. Louis hadn't come, so just me and my tubby selfish friend remained. Why didn't I stay with Louis? What energy did I, did Jim, did the

Professor, did Eon find to make us realise our own decisions are sometimes the best decisions?

"What I need is for you to give me a leg up, unless you want to be the hero and squeeze through those tiny tubes and grab the chocolate?" Jim growled.

I was shocked by his attitude towards me. I was helping him, I stood by him, yet he was being sarcastic to me. Why? I took two paces back and asked myself if I made the right decision. I breathed heavily and decided to answer Jim's snide comment, "No, you do it Jim, you're better at climbing than me, besides, I'm not really good with heights. If I climb all the way up there I'll get scared and you'd have to rescue me. And another thing, I'm quite partial to a bit of chocolate, I reckon I'd eat at least ten bars before you could blink."

"Willpower Jane, you should display willpower. You won't be catching me stuffing my face. Anyway, give me a leg up now, here goes." I always thought Jim was like myself and had an addiction to chocolate. He must have great strength of mind to resist his craving for a soft, succulent, creamy chocolate bar. Oh, the thought of it is unbearable, but also wonderful.

I watched tentatively as he pushed his way through a little hole and began climbing up inside. "Are you all right up there?" But he couldn't hear me. The glass casing that he'd crawled behind must have acted like a sound barrier. There were two layers of glass separated by about one centimetre of air. I wondered when I saw him up there whether there was any air inside the machine; would he die from a of lack of oxygen? I believe I too was suffering from the same disease that plagues Louis, that of paranoia.

Suddenly, out of nowhere the beast rushed passed me. The mystic ghost known as the Ssssylfia lingered within inches of my fluffy face. Louis wasn't around, what should I do? Jim saw it in front of me. He was making gestures with his paws and shouting silent words towards me. I guess I had to hear this ghost's riddle alone, so I spoke to it.

"Err, Hello Ssssylfia. Err, what do you want to say?"

DANGER! DANGER!
LURKS IN GREED
FIND THE ONE
IF JIM'S
TO BE FREED

It then just faded away. I turned towards Jim, he had chocolate all over his face and there were lots of wrappers around him.

"No!" I shouted. But it was no good. Jim had eaten over fourteen chocolate bars and looked quite ill. His greed was predicted by the Ssssylfia. I rushed, sort of panicking (I was scared and yet I'd done nothing) back up to Louis.

"Oh! Louis! Louis! A terrible thing has happened. The Ssssylfia spoke to me, it's Jim, he's going die…"

Russian Roulette - One false move you may regret

1. Greed

Yet again Jim had proved to everyone that he had no control. Yet again his immaturity, his silly, stupid side stood tall. His greed overcame any logic- we were in dire straits. Eon had left us, he had snubbed us to live with camouflaged rats and a clawless scratcher named Grimley. Max had vanished, probably snatched and a morning snack for a hungry scratcher. Jim ran away from Louis thinking he could save Max. I had fallen out with Louis because of his selfishness and sided with Jim. This problem had emerged because we were maturing and experiencing new things and this was possibly clouding our judgement. Louis was our leader, but because of his lies, his ignorance, his tunnel vision, he had allowed Jim's weakness to take him over. Jim's baby attitude and lust for chocolate may well have brought an end to his short life. Yet if only Louis had been sympathetic earlier then none of this would have happened. This new dilemma, this new horrible life-threatening situation could have been totally avoided. I rubbed my nose against Louis' nose, he was Jim's only hope and he really needed to help…

"Jim's trapped Louis, help him, and help me, please."

"If he should die, think only this of him, that there's a greedy mouse in a corner of a chocolate machine that will be forever in Louis' World! Ha! Ha!"

"Oh, don't say things like that Louis, you swine!" I cried. "Just help me get him out of there! Come on, quickly, there's not much time."

"What do you mean there's not much time?"

"I think the machine is air tight. Soon he won't be able to breathe. His annoying chit-chat will just become a memory. Memories are important, but nothing beats the real thing. Come on, you told me that once, where is your passion, your flair? Prove to me that you can be a hero once more."

"Jane, I don't live in this life to be a hero. I'm here for a purpose, for myself. I don't understand why everyone else is convinced that I'm doing all this for fame. It's not about that. Jim and the Professor know this, that's why they use me so much. If they get into any problems they think good old Louis will sort it out. How are they supposed to earn respect and trust if they continue to abuse my friendship?"

"So what are you going to do then? Are you just going to leave him in there to die?"

"Well, if what you say is true it's his own doing. He didn't have to gorge himself on that chocolate. You respected him for having the willpower not to, but now you see he was just using you, like he uses me. He strings us along you see. Firstly, we think he's coming round to our way of thinking then BAM! One act of selfishness and he's blown the respect in one swoop."

"So, should this act of foolishness cost him his life? I admit certain aspects of Jim's nature are subject to criticism, but that's who he is. A mouse like him can't change his character at the drop of a hat. It is written that the personality of a mouse is greater than the strength of any living thing."

"Well, even if it is, I'm sorry Jane, I don't want to help him. I can't believe there's no air in that chocolate machine. If there was no air surely all the chocolates would have gone off. And I know, well, I would put peanuts on it, that Jim wouldn't eat stale chocolate."

"That's not right at all. The chocolates are sealed so they don't need air; but he does! This isn't about your personal feelings anymore Louis. This is about the freedom of our group." I scampered right over to him and stared into his eyes. "Look at me Louis! Look deep into my eyes! Can you see tears? Can you see pain? Can you see that I'll never talk to you again if you let him die?"

"Jane! Jane! You are so blind. Yet, I feel for your soul. I will help Jim, but only because of you. It is written that blindness can warrant bad decisions as well as rendering us unable to see. Is it not more stupid, more blind to risk your life for a cause that will one day be your downfall?"

"Thank you, I think," I answered. I was so relieved that Louis would help.

We scampered back down the escalator together towards the chocolate machine. But wait! As we came around the corner onto the higher level I could see two machines on each side, but which higher level did we go to? I can't remember. Louis was not impressed by my unorganised plan. I had been rushing so much earlier that I hadn't paid attention to where we were.

"So, which machine is this tubby Jim stuck in?"

"Err, I? Err, I dunno?"

"What?"

"I can't remember?"

"Great!" We rushed towards the first machine. There didn't seem to be any scuff marks around it so we were stumped at the first hurdle.

"Wait!" I screamed, "this is a different type of machine. The one Jim's in had a large glass front where you could see all the chocolates on display. I remember because he said it was easier to get into than the others. But where is it?"

"Look Jane, are you sure it was down here on the higher levels and not in one of the higher tunnels?"

"It must have been… the Ssssylfia, that mystic ghost, spoke to me; it emerged from the blackness. Look, you go that way Louis and I'll go this way." I pointed at two different routes. I didn't understand what was happening.

Oh how I should have listened to my mother all those months ago. She always said to me that if ever I got caught in a tricky or dangerous situation to memorise the location. To look all around. To take note of the posters on the walls. The direction of the wind. The marks on the ground and the smell in the air. Suddenly my nose had picked up something. I closed my eyes and walked with the taste of the scent pulling me along. Yes! I was sure that I could smell Jim. There is no better, cleaner smell than that of Jim, although he also smelled fruity, like no it couldn't be but, like pineapple chunks.

BUMP! I walked straight into Louis. He fell onto the tracks straight into a puddle of pineapple juice.

"Watch where you're walking will you. Urr! This is the second time today that I've been covered in this nasty sticky stuff. Urr! It wreaks!" he squeaked.

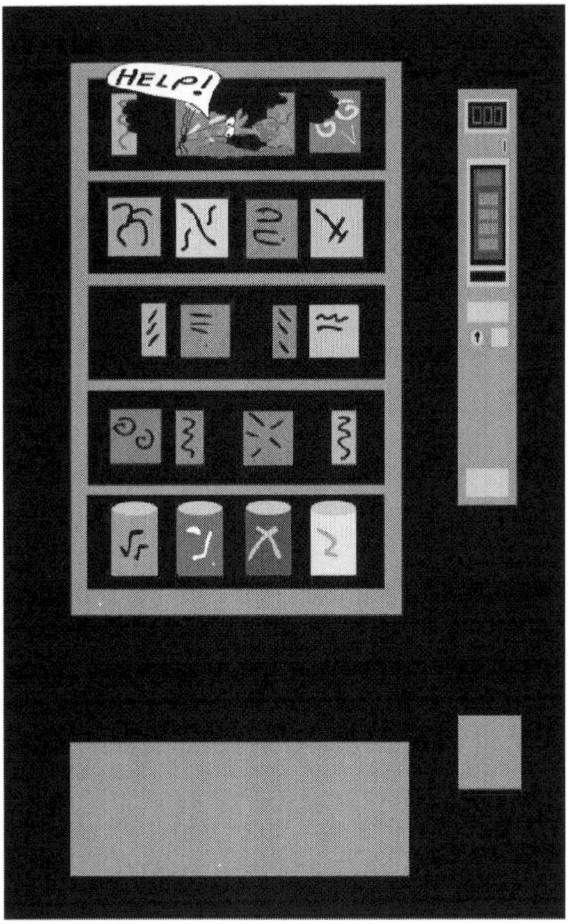

I looked all around, then I saw Jim out of the corner of my eye. I let out a deafening scream, “There he is!” He was lying on the top level of the machine in plain view. “Do you think he's all right? He isn’t moving.”

“I know he's there. I found him. Look! I was here first.”

“But do you think he's all right?”

“I dunno,” muttered Louis.

“That's a bit negative.”

“Look! Let's just try to get him out. Stop picking on me would you. I found him and it's going to be down to me as always to rescue him.”

“Well you don't have to be so enthusiastic,” I said sarcastically.

“Jane! Shhhhhh!”

“Sorry.”

Louis was in a bad mood. I sure hadn't helped matters when I’d accidentally pushed him in that fruity puddle.

“Jane, he's fine. He was laughing at me when you pushed me in that yucky stuff and has somehow managed to get his head stuck in that shelf unit, which I think serves him right. Ha! Ha!”

“Well you'll have to go in and get him won't you?”

“Why me?”

“Louis, come on, stop being lazy!”

“Lazy! That'll be the day.” He picked up the Professor's sack of inventions which Jim had left on the floor by the edge of the machine and started sifting through it.

“I wish the Professor could have had the common decency to have labelled his tablets rather just sticking his name on them. Still here goes.....” Louis pulled out a tablet and licked it. The tablet changed into a Max-Stepladder.

“That was clever Louis. How did you do that?”

“I don’t know, I thought it was going to be a Max-Crayon or Max-Pen but I suppose subconsciously I was thinking of steps to get him out and my imagination followed that tangent. Still, Jim was always a lucky mouse.” Louis again dipped his paw into the sack and pulled out a second tablet and licked it. This one turned into a piece of Max-Chalk. “Oh well, close enough.”

“What are you plotting?” I was confused. Louis was up to something but he wasn’t helping the matter by not telling me how we can free out foolish friend…

2. Mouse Code

A long time passed and Louis was frantically fiddling with the Professor's sack. It made me surer than ever that Max must've invented the tablets as he, unlike Louis was confident in their purpose. Louis stopped and looked sad. "I need to think of something… a way to communicate… got it! I know what to do! I just hope Jim can understand mouse code…"

⇉ ↑⇕▲➩ ◢⇕▶ ⇨△➩ ⇕↗⇨◢⤓

◢⇕▶ ▽↓↙↙◢

↙↓◀◀↙➩ ↘⇕▶▽➩⇲

He starting tapping and scraping the glass with the Max-Chalk. This took me back to my childhood. I remember having a lesson in mouse code when I was at school. Everyone was meant to listen, but some of our group never listened to what the mature mice had to say. They always scraped through the tests either by cheating or luck. I think Jim is one of these mice. He hardly ever listens to what Louis is saying. How foolish he is. I do hope I'm wrong. But Jim has been kissed by the gift of luck; if fortune was ever to follow one mouse around all his life that mouse would be Jim.

"When did you learn this mouse code?" I asked.

"It was when I was very young," explained Louis. "It was forced onto us. Many of the rodents that I grew up with didn't want to learn other languages. They thought it was unwise. So what if you learn how to communicate with other creatures, they'll never help a starving mouse, that's what they used to say. But my uncle, Stephen, helped me understand. He said it wasn't just for mice, it was for all rodent-kind. It is written that the more you know the better you become. Languages of other species are very complicated. You can't expect them to be easy. Nothing that's worth anything is easy. Take those chocolate bars that Jim's eaten. Some of those chocolate bars contain nuts. The different nuts are from different areas. So the chocolate bars, in a way are different flavours mixed-up. And is it not a fact that Jim's lust for a peanut drove him to succumb to the temptations of these chocolates. I believe the chocolates are a skilled plan to deceive self-conscious rodents. It is written that too many peanuts spoil the broth. I believe this broth is the one now known as Crimson Pigs. If ever we meet such a rodent we'll be in for a bumpy ride. Some mice say he is a crossbred gerbil and guinea pig. I believe this to be the truth. Some mice say he is all seeing and all knowing. I too believe this to be the truth. But he hates authority. If we rescue Jim today and meet this Crimson Pigs with Jim in such an arrogant mood our days will surely be numbered. It was my uncle that taught me mouse code. He said one day it would save a friend's life. Maybe that time is now…"

"Let's hope it works."

Jim started to move. I saw his head juddering about. He was struggling on the top shelf. One false move and he'd be a goner for sure. As we watched we could see the pain in his eyes as he forced his fat face out of the wedged position...

POP!

He was free. He still looked very tubby. He was still covered in chocolate. We watched him as he opened his mouth and took out an enormous peanut, by far the biggest one I've ever seen. He reached out towards the glass and began tapping and scraping as Louis had done earlier.

⌃↑⇨◀➔▽ ⇦⇨◀◀⇨△←

⇉ ↑⇨◀⇨ ⇨ ⇦↕↘⇦ ↕← ⇨↑↕⇨

↕↙⇨◀⇨⤓ ↔⇨▽◀◢⇲

"What is it Louis? What's he trying to say?"

"I can't quite make it out. It's something like… THAT'S B..UT.TER? Then it says.. BO..J M..B. NAS… " Louis started writing the letters on the ground with the Max-Chalk as Jim tapped them out, but they didn't make any sense to me.

"There he goes again look!" I squeaked.

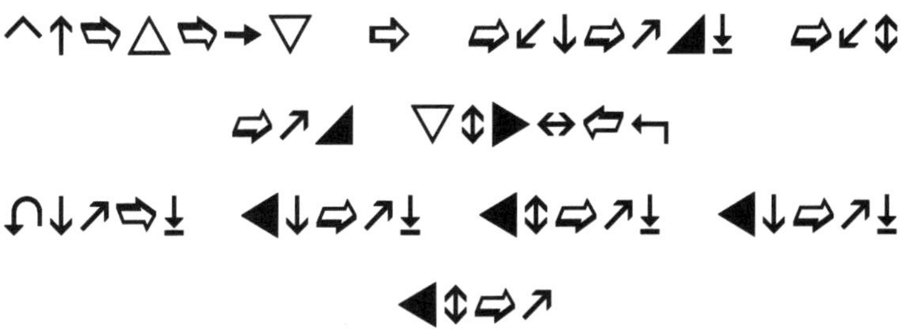

"What is it?"

"Shhh! Jane. It's tricky F.U.N..N.Y… CLO.. CKY SOU..N..D… T...I...C..KK.. T..O..C..K..." Louis wrote more letters down.

"WHAT DOES IT SAY?" I shouted at the top of my lungs. It was such a penetrating squeal that it attracted the attention of unpredictables. We could hear some foot steps coming down the escalator.

“Quickly, let's hide on the track,” he bellowed. Louis and myself signalled towards Jim and jumped down to the tracks out of sight of the unpredictables.

“So Louis, what did Jim say?” I whispered to him.

“He talks of a bomb. Although his spelling is somewhat wrong. I think he's trying to say that there's a bomb in the chocolate machine with him and that it's ticking. That would explain why there are no unpredictables down here. Unpredictables don't like bombs,” he whispered back.

“So what's a bomb then?” I asked.

“It could mean one of two things. Either an explosive device or a large amount of something.”

“Is that good or not?”

“I thought you were quite up to date with your reading Jane? Have you not read the Sacred Scroll that tells of a mouse known as Guy who, with an explosive device, blows up buildings.”

“So it's a bad thing then.”

“Bad? It's hideous.”

“Oh look, those unpredictables have disappeared again. Let's.....” I was about to come out of hiding but Louis stopped me.

"Wait Jane! Look over there, do you see what I see…?"

Louis pointed to a large shadow. The more we looked at it the bigger it got. Then relief struck us, for it was the Professor. He scampered around the corner. He looked quite happy but then again he nearly always did. We climbed up the Max-Stepladder onto the higher level to greet our spectacled friend…

3. Tug-of-War

"Hello Professor, where have you been?" I said hugging him. Louis then hugged him too but Max pushed him away.

"Urrr, you're all sticky Louis. Nasty. Yucky. Now where was I? Oh I couldn't resist you see. I found this lovely grassy hill. It was a long way down the concrete lake, but it was by far the best run I've had for ages. It was nice to get some fresh air in my lungs rather than be stuck down here all the time. Although it was starting to become rather cold, so I thought I'd come back. Anyway, where's Jim?"

"You see that machine over there," Louis pointed to the chocolate machine, "he's stuck in there."

"Ha! Ha! Is he! Ha! Ha!"

"It's not funny Professor," I moaned. "He can't communicate because of the thickness of the glass so Louis' talking to him via the mouse code method. Did you ever learn that?"

"Yeah, a long time ago though. Hey, you'd better watch out you know, there's an awful lot of unpredictables about. I think they're safe ones though. I can't see any earrings. Hey, where did that Max-Stepladder come from? Have you been dipping into my sack of inventions without asking?"

"You weren't around to ask were you? Anyway, you left your precious sack upstairs by the railings, and as possession is nine tenths of the law, they're mine," grinned Louis as he pulled the sack tightly to his chest.

"Louis! Give them back!"

"No!"

"Come on give them back!"

"No, I found them." A nasty tug-of-war match started to flare up between them. The sack would go one way, then the other. As they pulled at it, it stretched and weirdly expanded in size. Everything was brought to a head when Jim started tapping again.

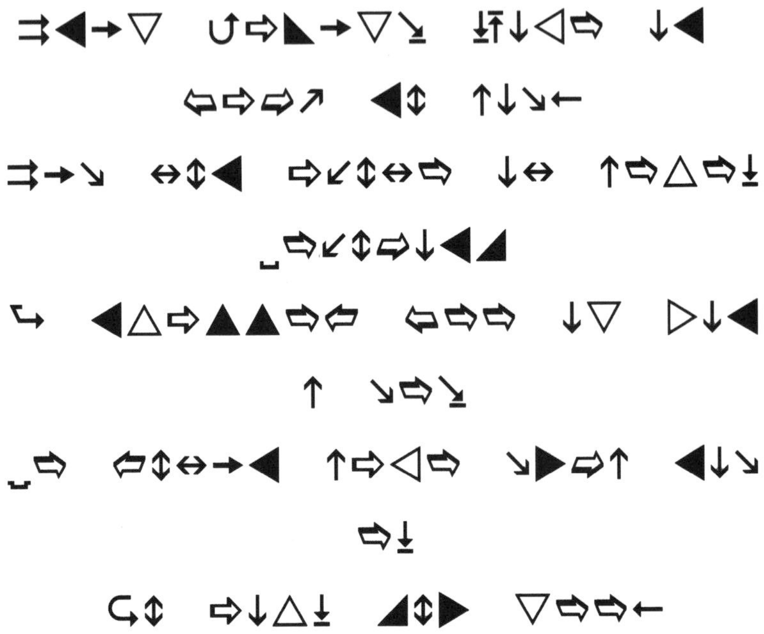

“What's he saying now?” I asked.

“Err… Not.. ALO…… NE. T...I.. M… E.. V… BE… M...I...N...S… I think,” replied Louis.

“So what's that supposed to mean?” moaned Max. “He's making up his own mouse code, unless… give me my sack, I've got an idea?” The Professor dipped again into his sack, licked a tablet and it changed into a Max-Translator.

"What does that do?"

"Well Louis, unless I'm very much mistaken this letter *V* is from another language. It's just a case of finding out which one." The Professor sat on the floor and started tapping numbers and letters into his invention. I just hoped he'd solve this riddle soon. I guess the Ssssylfia was right then. It spoke of the *ONE* needing to be found to free Jim. Maybe the *ONE* was this letter *V*.

"Jane, you'd better keep a look out by the escalators in case any of those unpredictables come back, whilst we try and communicate with Jim again."

"Okay. I'll see you in a bit then." I scampered to where Louis asked for me to go. I could see him from where I was standing. He rushed up to the glass again, he then started tapping on it…

⇉▽ ␣ ◀↑➩ ◀↓↘➩ ◢⇕▶ ↑⇨
◁➩ ◀⇕ ➩▽➪⇨▲➩↴
⇉▽ ◀↑➩△➩ ⇨ ⇦⇕↘⇦ ↓↔ ◀↑
➩△➩↴
⇉▽ ◀↑⇨◀ ▷↑⇨◀ ◢⇕▶➞△➩
▽⇨◢↓↔→↴

I really should have paid more attention in class. I understood the odd letter but the majority of it was a muddle… sadness.

"I've got it!" screamed the Professor, "it means either four or five! It must mean he's got either four or five minutes to live. Come on there's no time to lose. Louis, tap on the glass and tell him to risk everything. If he doesn't make it out he'll die anyway… Go on, scrape and tap now!"

⤓⤒⇨◀ ⇕▶◀ ⇔⇕▷ ⇦⇨←⇕△⇨

⇉◀ ⇨◣▲↙⇕⇦⇨▽←

"That's it… I've told him he's got to get out before it explodes as there's no way we can deactivate it from here."

Louis signalled towards me and I rushed back, leaving my post unattended. I looked at my friends on the higher level frantically trying to rescue Jim, but it was no good. He smiled at me through the glass. He seemed almost complacent about death. He squashed his left paw against the glass, it flattened his fluffy skin. Tears started to roll down his cheeks, and down mine too. I couldn't believe there was nothing we could do. Was this the last I would see of him? Would my last memory of him be that of a fat mouse who went inside a machine in a bid to rescue the Professor who didn't need rescuing? The fool. I imagined seeing the words written across his tombstone.

THE FOOL!
HERE LIES
JIM AMADEUS JERBIL
HE CAME
HE JOKED
HE FOOLED
HE MADE MISTAKES
THAT COST HIM
HIS LIFE
2011 – 2012

It makes me think of a story he told me once about how he used to go hiding in a park with two of his brothers. They liked hiding. It was their favourite game. It was on a cold winter's day. It was the day before his first birthday. First month that is. He told me how they'd all hide in the park as usual, letting the more mature mice hunt for them. They could see in their faces that these older mice didn't like playing this game, yet they allowed them the freedom of youth; to explore avenues of comradeship. I guess that's why Jim doesn't like

Louis, as he seems too mature. I believe he wants to relive his life with his brothers, which of course he can't do. Anyway, during these winter months the pond would freeze. I guess the adventure always lit Jim's life up. But this day he'll remember today I'm sure of it. This pond that froze opened up new doors. New hiding places. The brothers thought, because of the freeze, it would be a tease to sneak out onto the ice. To slip and slid. To hide. Their foolish games! That's what the head mouse said. Three young mice with hopes ahead. Three young mice filled with fun. Three young mice knocked down to one. Never did the mature ones ever see them playing again. Jim said it was ironically funny in a way. Until the day of the funeral. His happy smile, his glow was gone. It was as if some one had snuffed out his light. The fun was over and it opened his eyes, alas too late for his brothers paid with their lives…

"Jane! Jane! Stop staring at him, he hasn't got much time."

"Oh, sorry. I was just thinking." We watched as Jim tapped on the glass one last time.

⇉➞↙↙ ◀△◢ ⇨↔⇦ →⇨◀ ⇕▶◀

▷↓◀↑

␣⇨↙⇕⇨↓◀◢➞▽ ↑⇨↙▲⇲

He then waved and scrambled down from one shelf to another. There was an odd yellow and black ghost-like shape with him emitting a strange buzzing noise. We watched as he couldn't quite reach the second last level so he had to force his way into the machine. The rest of the story about his escape will have to come from his own diary of events, I guess.

"Look, he's disappearing in," I cried. "This may be the last time we'll see him alive. There's so many things that I should have said to him. Oh how foolish I was not to tell him how I really felt. I remember once, quite a long time ago, I saw him standing by himself aimlessly gazing into the night sky. He told me that he had always wondered what it would be like to be a star, a glistening, sparkling energy far away from the torment and greed of our world. He also told me that he thought the stars were his parents and their parents before them. He always thought that when you died your soul would float into the sky and join its family. The stars would be windows looking back onto the world. Each window giving a different view. A different aspect of life. There were thousands upon thousands of stars. Each cluster, each galaxy, would be an entire generation. He often wondered if this were true. He often asked me if I really did believe in the Sacred Scrolls. It is written that if life is everlasting why do our loved ones have to die?

That was the scroll that annoyed him the most. For it wasn't an answer, a solution, like the others; it was a question. Surely the scrolls needn't ask questions. They were made so that every rodent had a belief. What was the point of a scroll which read that life goes on even if you die? He said he didn't think it was appropriate. It made a mockery of all the scrolls. It's more like the kind of scroll that you Louis, in an annoying mood, would have written. If such a rodent was allowed to write such things then the whole scroll dream is nothing but a shambles. He was very bitter about them. I used to watch him sit on the hill side of a town very near here actually. That town was called Primrose Hill. There was no mechanical beast there, I guess that makes it a tad more secluded. It's cut off from the real world if you like. Sometimes I used to think that Jim was cut off from the real world. He was selfish beyond all belief. He told me another story involving his two brothers, the two that died in the pond. It had happened about one week before. They only just escaped death that time. He said that he should have known it was coming really. The others were a fraction more naive than him you see, they were young and innocent. Innocence is always going to be a danger to every young mouse."

"Jane, is there a point to this story?" asked a tired looking Louis. He was lying on the edge of the higher level in exactly the same position as he had before. He said he was listening with his eyes closed again. It was as though history was repeating itself. Bizarre it was, very, very bizarre.

"Yes, this story is laced with meaning although I never really noticed it before. I never thought I could tell long stories. I always thought that I was the listener, the quiet one who just nodded now and then. Still, without Jim and all his exploits and experiences I'd have nothing to say. It was the energy inside him that I liked the most. His instincts, his immaturity; these are the characteristics that made Jim different to others. I will miss him," I sighed. A small tear rolled down my face and trickled down one of my whiskers. I was dejected.

"So what's the point then?" grumbled Louis.

"Err, I dunno, I've forgotten."

Meanwhile the Professor was starting to become aggressive, "Come on then Louis, and give me my sack back! Just because I've sorted Jim out doesn't....."

"You haven't sorted him have you? He's still stuck in there you fool!" moaned Louis. This started off a slanging match between them. They were pushing and shoving at the sack again.

"Give it back!" screamed the Professor.

"No!" bleated Louis.

"Come on!"

"No!"

"Come on you.....!"

"No, it's mine."

"No it's not."

"Is too."

"Is not."

"Is."

"Isn't."

"Yes it is."

"No it isn't."

"Come on you two break it up," I moaned and suddenly I'd become a referee in their petty squabble over ownership…

4. Kangaroo Court

"Look let's do this like a courtroom drama. Jane, you're the judge and both lawyers okay? I'm the innocent and you Louis, are the guilty!" announced the Professor.

"No! No! I'm the innocent, you're the one who's guilty."

"No! The Professor's right. It was originally his sack so he is kind of the innocent party here."

"Favouritism, that's what it is."

“Look Louis stop complaining. Let's get on with the trial. I just hope it doesn't take too long.”

We used an old bean tin as our dock. Firstly the Professor entered and I said “Do you Professor Max Clifton Jerbil swear to speak the truth, the whole truth and nothing but the truth so help us all.”

“I do.”

"It is the 28th February which you need to tell us about. At exactly 12:30pm you were seen by myself trying to catch peanuts off the unpredictable shopkeeper who ran our lives. Correct?”

“Err, I think so.”

“What! Answer the question with a definite yes or no. Clear?” I shrieked.

“Err, yes. Yes it will be clear and yes I was trying to catch peanuts from the party mentioned.”

“Now, what I would like to know is what you were doing between the times of 12:31pm and 12:37pm exactly?......Come on, speak or I'll hold you in contempt of court.”

“Err. I remember catching six peanuts then hiding them under the wheel with all my other ones, Madam.”

“Is this all that you did?”

“Yes, Madam. That's all.”

“Did you have any witnesses?”

"Well Eon saw me, but he's not with us now so it doesn't count."

"That's either very unlucky or very clever of you Professor."

"Is that it?"

"Yes, you may step down… I'm now calling the guilty party to approach the dock." Louis scampered over towards the area sectioned off, but seemed in the mood to complain.

"Err, aren't I innocent until proven guilty, Madam?"

"Not in my courtroom you're not," I screamed.

"Damn!" Louis mumbled.

"So, do you Louise Jerbil also known as Louis the Furred agree to tell the truth, the whole truth and nothing but the truth so help us all?"

"I do."

"At 12:30pm on 28th February you were seen by me running on that wheel in our sawdust prison. You were facing the shop door I believe. Correct."

"Err, correct Madam, but I was…"

"A simple yes is sufficient. Now can you tell me your whereabouts between the times of 12:31pm and 12:37pm exactly?"

"Was that when me and Eon were discussing escaping?"

"Are you asking me or telling me?"

“I'm telling.”

"Right. You too may step down. I'm going take a short recess of fourteen seconds and then we'll continue.” I waved my gavel, (a little hammer) and struck the higher level…

THUD!

I ran over to the spilled pineapple juice and had a good lick. Louis joined me. I think he was trying to be courteous. Trying to swing the result in his favour, the cheating toad!

“Right!” I whacked the gavel down again. This sound meant the court was again in session.

THUD!

“On the evidence I've heard it seems that one of you is lying. The clear facts are as follows. The Professor has always been to my knowledge an inventor. Whether or not he’s capable of inventing his story is one deciding factor. Louis is honest as the day is young. I've known him all my life. If he says that the sack of inventions is really his because of the nine tenths of the law scenario, then I have to go… ”

“WAIT!” cried Jim. He was free. “What are you saying? Are you saying that the inventor doesn’t own the inventions or doesn’t deserve them? Where is the justice here I ask myself? The Professor has always told me that if you believe in youself then you’ll escape all dangers, this of course involves being called a fraud. If they are not his inventions then I’m dead, and I’m not am I, although you all thought I would be.”

"Jim! You're right of course. For although I feel that his unorganised attitude at leaving them lying around means he shouldn't own them, that's no excuse for me to take something that's not mine to take," sighed Louis.

"Great Louis, I thought you'd won my prize then. You had a *one-in-six* chance of getting away with blue murder then and my family would be turning in their graves if you'd got away with it," grinned Max.

"With the evidence swinging into Louis' favour I am stunned. Yet the confession that Louis is willing to accept Jim's plea bargain means I hereby order that you Max Clifton Jerbil, the Professor, that you, as has now been decided by this court room, are the rightful owner of the inventions sack and all the little tablets inside it. They are yours and yours alone."

"Superb!" he squeaked.

"This court is now adjourned… Jim, I'm so happy you're alive," I said. I hugged him, well we all did. It was a shock to have him back. I struck my gavel down again, the courtroom closed. My acting days were over and my friendship days had begun once more…

5. Jim's Exaggerated Escape

"So Jane, what's this odd story you talk of? I don't understand how you came to believe the sack couldn't be the Professor's?" asked Jim. He was back to his normal chirpy self; it was so lovely to have him back.

"Well, it's a bit complicated but here goes. The Professor we all know wore a glove to catch his peanuts but he never told us about this until after we'd escaped. So how do we know it wasn't just an ordinary gardening glove? If he'd made hundreds of inventions why did he keep them a secret? Unless he discovered this bag of inventions later when we entered Louis' World, and as it was Louis' World, shouldn't everything we find belong to him? If you find lost property you should hand it in to the local authorities and only if no rodent claims it after one month does the item or items legally become the property of the finder."

"I've always had this sack though," muttered the Professor.

"I do remember once that… I'm… yes… pretty sure he had that sack in the prison," replied a thoughtful looking Jim.

"Thanks for lying," the Professor mumbled to him discreetly.

"Yeah, well, now you owe me one...."

"So Jim, how did you… oh no, wait! We've got to get out of here?" yelled Louis.

"Eh?" quizzed Jim.

"You know that bomb's about to blow up."

"What bomb?"

"What?" asked a confused looking Louis.

"I told you that in mouse code that *V* was the name of a bee I met. I didn't say anything about a bomb."

"A bee? And crocodiles too no doubt! I've heard enough!"

"So we're safe then? Oh what a relief," I replied. I decided to ask Jim his story of how he escaped from the chocolate machine if he didn't mind. I knew it would be a far-fetched story but I was looking for a pleasant end to an unpleasant day.

"So how did you get out?" I asked Jim.

"Well, it was an adventure in a style that you've never seen or heard before."

"Here we go, total fiction time commences," growled Louis. He had his head in his paws, was sitting upright by the edge of the tracks and looked miserable.

"Look Louis if you don't want to hear it, go over there and wait for your Ssssylfia thing," he replied, pointing to a metal seat.

"I'll join you if you don't mind Louis," moaned the Professor, "I can't stand the way he exaggerates his stories. I wonder how many alligators or crocodiles live in that chocolate machine. Ha! Ha!" They both scurried over towards the metal seats and had a doze.

"We are listening, but with our eyes closed," joked Louis.

"So go on then Jim, tell me the story of your escape and don't leave anything out except the lies," I said.

"Jane, would I lie to you?" He looked deep into my eyes and smiled.

"No, I guess you wouldn't."

"Right, where to begin. I believe it all started when I was born.... Ha! Ha! Only joking, you know that I wouldn't go that far back. I remember watching this ghost thing come out of the blackness. I couldn't speak to you if you remember. The glass inside was very thick and seemed to possess two layers. I saw you speak to it but I didn't know what you, or indeed it, was saying. What did it say?"

"It said: Danger! Danger! Lurks in greed, find the *ONE* if Jim's to be freed," I replied.

"How bizarre. So what's this *ONE* then?"

"I don't know?"

"Oh. Anyway, after it had gone I found that my hunger was more powerful than my willpower. I'd eaten loads of chocolate bars without being conscious of the fact that I had. It was strange you know, to look down and see a podgy tummy that I never thought I had or would indeed get. I still can't explain why I was eating them without really thinking. I have always been the kind of mouse who likes to chew my food, not to rush it as if it's not there at all. Odd eh? Anyway, about my escape. I noticed the trapped bee and informed Louis using mouse code. I then tried to make it down to the lowest level. I thought that if I made any sudden moves it would jolt this bee and it may have stung me so I was cautious, you know. I could only make it to the third from bottom shelf. The next step was just a little too big to risk going down, so I decided then and there to head into the labyrinth so to speak. It was enormous inside. It had one of those virtual reality looks. Actually, come to think of it, it was totally real. It was a cavern of mysterious pathways. I felt as though one false move would trigger the bee! Anyway, there were six paths ahead of me. I couldn't tell which one was safe. I was pretty scared. Then I remember I was going to take the first path on the left until I saw a strange shape lurking in the shadows. I thought at first it was an alligator, but then I thought how could an alligator hide inside this chocolate machine? I've never heard of alligators using these kinds of places as cool hide outs. So, I then thought it might be a baby crocodile. You see, there is a zoo in London's premier park. I reckon that some of the crocodiles' eggs were smuggled out by a gang of hamsters. You know what hamsters are like, one chance of wealth and there all out to get it. Crocodile skin sells very well in the market stalls around this town. Jane! Jane! Wake up, you can't sleep, this story has only just begun."

"Yeah, that's what I'm afraid of."

"Anyway, I believe that these hamsters regularly stole crocodile's eggs from the zoo and a lot of these sinister monsters are free and roaming in the canals of this fine city."

"So, let me get this straight, you reckon that a baby crocodile has managed to climb into the chocolate machine, right?" I answered. Louis warned me of his far-fetched stories, but at least he was alive and back to his normal lying self.

"Well, if you say it without the proper context of course it will sound unbelievable. Let me finish please. Right, these hamsters lost a sack of eggs. Is it not written that bad management equals a sloppy performance? And every mouse knows that hamsters aren't the best organisers. *V* told me a gang of six hamsters have kidnapped the 2nd heir to the throne of Jerboa?"

"Who's *V*?" I mumbled. He'd totally lost me.

"I'm coming to that… where was I? Oh yeah… I really hate hamsters and I hate crocodiles too. Anyway, obviously I didn't go that way. I took the next path. It was very twisty. But the more I forced myself inside, the tighter it got. I remember thinking that I shouldn't have eaten quite so many chocolate bars; still it was amusing in a way. Then suddenly I came across a wiry bridge. Millions and millions of wires as far as my eyes could see and then I began to hear a faint buzzing sound. What was it I thought? It seemed to be coming from a row of yellow and black wires, but these weren't wires, as under a plastic coating I could see a young trapped bee. I prodded him to see if he was alive, and he was. His name was Velocity but his nickname was *V* because he was so speedy. He said Victoria, his queen was probably panicking with worry. He asked me if I could cut him out of the plastic. I tried. Well, a mouse has got to do what a mouse has got to do. When he was free he told me that he'd been stuck in their for ages. His queen told him he should be hibernating during the cold months, but as he was curious, he took a close look at the chocolate machine and somehow became trapped. He said he had been in there three months and only woke when I poked him. He said it felt like he was asleep for maybe three seconds and not three months as time races by when bees hibernate. Anyway *V* had these large pads on his knees. He said if I wanted he'd help me get out but I'd have to tie my whiskers round his knees. Normally, he told me, he lands on his knees but recently he had lost full control of his wings and he was crash landing too much, hence the pads; as you can see this was a tad worrying for me. But his plan worked. I got a little bump on my head when he landed on me but I was safe, if that Max-Stepladder hadn't been in the way I'd have been unscathed. Anyway, I said goodbye to *V* and he buzzed off."

Jim continued to rant on with his made-up story of escape. I liked having him back, but the lies and the twisted stories of his imagination were at times, annoying.

"The way out was quite easy really," grinned Jim. "It's funny isn't it how so many things are so easily solved. All he did was fly down the money hole; this lead to what I thought was a blocked route. He told me some unpredictables, normally the ear-ringed type, chew a substance known as gum and they think it funny to block the holes like these with it. We tasted it. It tasted very faintly of mint. Together we picked at it and managed to dig a large enough hole to slide through. I tied myself back on and we were out. I had to fly out with him because just before the doorway to freedom there was a sheer drop, no mouse in a million years could have jumped that crevasse. And here I am, cool eh? I escaped, ate a whole load of chocolate and managed to make a new friend in the process. That's one to tell my grand children when I'm old and grey, past my better days."

"Is that it?" I yawned.

"Yeah. Game, set and match," he grinned.

6. Hibernation Theory

"Louis! Louis! He's finished. You can come back now," I shouted and with that Louis and the Professor came over to us. They looked worn out. I bet those metal seats were uncomfortable. Still we were reunited again, all four of us and eager to find out our futures.

"So now what then?" asked an eager Jim.

"Now we… "

Suddenly the mechanical beast rushed passed followed by the Ssssylfia.

THE ONE HOLDS
POSSESSIONS
UNLIKE ME
FULFILMENT
IS YOUR KEY

"Louis! What's that supposed to mean? It's going on about the *ONE* again, one what?" I asked.

"Err, I'm sure it will make sense later."

"I think I understand how the Rat-Routes work now Louis," said an alert looking Jim.

"What?" quizzed Louis.

"If say I slept for three months and awoke in the same state as if I'd been sleeping for only three seconds, then time would pass by, yet I wouldn't miss it."

"What are you babbling about?" moaned Louis.

"Hibernation. A bee told me there are lots of things that make sense when you stand back and review them from a different perspective."

"Rubbish!" cursed Louis. "I reckon we should head for Bell-Sized Park and find Paul, unless we get delayed in our mission again… "

As the thoughts and memories continued to race inside my mind I felt my life had finally begun. Jim had been to Bell-Sized Park but what secrets did he miss? We all waited for the mechanical beast, jumped on the bumper and it pulled away into another dark tunnel of our lives…

A spy will open closed eyes -
He makes the world seem bigger
yet he is much smaller

1. The Search for Paul

I was more scared than usual. After the exploits of nearly witnessing the end of Jim's life, after seeing the Professor come through a horrid courtroom drama and knowing that our leader Louis, wasn't really that good a leader after all, worried me. Yes, the Professor had his sack of inventions back. Yes Jim was safe. His tales of crocodiles were inflated but imagine what it would be like if one day they were true. He said he met a new ally, a yellow and black bee called *V* who worn knee pads as *V* was clumsy at landing. Yes, maybe the days are becoming stranger but the excitement and sheer drama outweighs any fears in our search for Dark Energy. For I think this force is beginning to show itself to us. It isn't something we can see as such, or touch or taste, but there is a passion in our blood that is willing us to move forward. I may just be getting the wrong end of the stick here, but maybe the Dark Energy is all around us, because we have the ability to control our emotions. Now though we had to direct our focus away from what had happened and concentrate on what might happen. Jim, who could be lying (after all he is good at that) has said he dropped the pecan we think is Paul in Bell-Sized Park. As we sit here on the bumper of the beast, unsure as to why the Rat-Routes are no different to unpredictable routes, we head to a town where a mouse-eating spider lives. A horrid place that is more terrifying than the rest and that's where we are going! The Ssssylfia speaks again of the *ONE* yet as usual none of us know what the *ONE* is. I know I've said this before and I don't want to come across as too negative or too repetitive, but I wonder sometimes, should I have stayed in the warmth and security of that pet shop in Clapham all those days ago…

"We wandered together after listening to that ghost, it floated around us high above the tracks, when all at once we watched it disappear and thoughts of danger lingered in the air," chanted Louis. He was waving his paws in the air as usual.

"Louis! Please stop your idle babbling, we need to find out what this *ONE* thing is. Have you got any idea?"

"I don't know what it is. Maybe this Ssssylfia is the *ONE* that the Sacred Scrolls speak off. Maybe I'm not the *ONE* at all. Maybe our group, our gang is not the *ONE*. Maybe it's another gang. Maybe, who knows?"

"Louis! You're not helping us very much you know," argued Jim. He was sitting with his legs dangling off the edge of the bumper and pulling his longest whisker far away from his face and pinging it back into its normal curly shape.

We sat there in the blackness and saw the Ssssylfia again creeping up behind us, it was quite faint but it was definitely there. Jim perked up when he saw it and tried to reach out and grab it, but his paw just passed through the shimmering mist as if there were no substance to it at all.

REMEMBER THAT GANGS
GATHER FOR TREASON
AND GAMES OCCUR
FOR REASONS

"So Louis, what does that mean what other gang? And don't say you don't know because you said the *ONE* might be another gang too!" groaned Jim.

Suddenly the Ssssylfia appeared and spoke a second time, but this wasn't a pleasant riddle and scared Jim more than ever.

SEEK ADVICE
WHEN FULL
OR BE EATEN

"So Louis, who's gonna be eaten? I don't wanna be eaten!" He was really upset and I didn't blame him. Louis was telling us one thing, then another, then another. It was difficult to work out which version was true, if any.

"That's because I don't know the answer Jim," sighed Louis. "I do however, reckon that the answer is staring us in the face, that it's there but we just can't see it. I think when we find it we'll know it though. It is written that when you find what you're looking for it's the bee's knees."

"Bees knees you say," answered Jim in a confused manner.

"Yes Jim, the bee's knees."

"I met a bee. He was called *V*. He wore knee pads because his flying wasn't going very well. He said he sprained one of his wings or something."

"What are you talking about?" asked Louis. He was equally confused.

"Well if you listened to me you'd know. I met a bee in that chocolate machine."

"Oh and crocodiles too no doubt. It is written in the Sacred Scrolls of Jerboa that constant lying causes sore throats. You'll get a sore throat soon, and it won't be very comfortable, then you'll come moaning back to me about how sorry you are, etc, etc… "

"What?"

"Moaning."

"I don't moan."

"Yes you do, all the time."

"Do I? Do I moan Jane?"

"I'm afraid so. Jim Moany-Mood Amadeus Jerbil will be scribbled on your tombstone."

"Err, sorry," Jim mumbled as he sulked on his own at the corner of the bumper. He was so close to the edge that he almost fell off.

It was boring sitting on that bumper and watching things. Nobody was saying anything; we just sat there in our own little worlds. Louis had his arms crossed and looked in the opposite direction from Jim. Jim just seemed to stare at his feet. He had dirty toes, black from the chocolate and dust mix. The Professor had decided to lie down. He'd tied his whiskers around the bumper, but unlike before he'd tied a easy looser knot; and I was just being myself. I was just gazing at the unpredictables at each higher level, watching as some went and new ones came and went.

"We have to get off here," bellowed Louis. He spoke with authority in his voice but his unruly shouting was unpleasant and upsetting as we all nearly jumped out of our skin. "It's Cam's Den again. We need to change beast and head for Bell-Sized Park as it is via a different route. If we stay on this beast we'll end up at the end-of-the-tracks again."

"Yeah well we don't want to go there again do we," answered an unhappy Jim.

"Come on then… stop dawdling you lot, it's this way," he said, as he pointed towards some steps. We all followed like lambs to the slaughter or bees to the honey, which ever way you want to put it.

"Look," Louis shouted. "There's a mechanical beast now! Quickly! Come on!" We all climbed on board the rear bumper and sat there waiting and worrying about what lay ahead.

This beast was a bit cleaner than the previous one. Jim said the old ones puff out smoke, and that's what the Ssssylfia is, smoke.

"Jim the Ssssylfia isn't smoke," complained Louis.

"So what is it then?"

"It's a White Energy from our thoughts," grinned Louis. He was being smug as usual and Jim was getting annoyed as usual.

"So let me get this straight. We are looking for Dark Energy and find White Energy, how weird. But why can't this ghost be Dark Energy, after all it comes from the blackness which is dark. I don't understand?" sulked Jim.

"The Ssssylfia is an answer. A helping paw in the struggle to find our purpose. There won't be smoke coming out of these as they're run by electricity."

"But I've found my purpose… see… " Jim poked Louis in the eye with his left finger from his right paw.

"Hey! Don't do that it's not nice… wait a minute… where's your other fingers gone?" asked Louis.

Louis looked at Jim but he was being mischievous. He had one paw behind his back and seemed to be fiddling with his other paw. Then Jim dropped a fluffy thing on the ground in front of Louis and looked even more shifty than usual.

"Eh?" Jim looked down and he had somehow lost three fingers. How did that happen? How can he lose three fingers? We all started to hunt around the bumper, then Louis said, "Is that them?" pointing at three fluffy stalks in front of us.

"No! But it is odd, I'll give you that," giggled Jim. "But surprise! Ha! Ha!" Jim rolled out his paw and lo and behold he'd taped them up, thus giving the impression of his loss. The three stalks were chocolate finger biscuits covered with fluff.

"Why you… " Louis attempted to grab Jim's fingers, but he slipped and he to cut his leg on a sharp piece of metal.

"Ha! Ha!" giggled Jim.

Suddenly the beast we were sitting on picked up speed and we held on for dear life. We thought a mad hamster must have gained control but we weren't sure. The beast then seemed to rush passed Bell-Sized Park without stopping; why? "What's going on?" I asked Louis.

"I'm not sure," he replied. "Maybe there's a bomb here too! Hang on, what are we going to do about that other bomb, we can't just leave it there. Maybe we should inform the unpredictables."

"Who's going to listen to us, we're mice. No unpredictable will take us seriously you fool. Anyway, what bomb are you talking about?" argued Jim.

"The one in the chocolate machine."

"I didn't know that?" snarled Jim.

"But it was you who told us it was there?" moaned Louis back to him.

"No I didn't."

"Yes you did."

"Did I?"

"You said in mouse code that there was a ticky sound and there was a nasty bomb."

"No! I said I ate a bomb of chocolate. And the ticky sound wasn't a clock because as it got louder it was a bee. A buzzy one named *V*."

"What?" snapped Louis.

"*V*. Actually his full name was *Velocity* because he was speedy."

"You do talk some rubbish. Never mind… I want to try something, if that place blows up, unpredictables die, it would make me feel sad."

"Well I wouldn't feel sad," moaned Jim. "Those unpredictables wouldn't diffuse a bomb for us you know, not that there was one. If we were in a sinking ship in the middle of the Great Sea the unpredictables wouldn't care. It's like that thing I read in that unpredictables' newspaper."

"What are you on about?" I asked.

"Shhh! I read that an unpredictable sunk his boat in the Great Sea and millions of the unpredictable substance known as money was used for his rescue. Now my uncle and his closest friends were in a boat once. Regent's Park pond I think it was called. Anyway, they were happily sunbathing and fishing when an unpredictable's boat rammed into them. It was being driven by a young ear-ringed type. Anyway, he just left my uncle and his friends to die. I ask you, is this fair? Are these unpredictables worthy of our trust? I doubt it. One unpredictable, risking his life doing a silly thing that is totally his fault and responsibility, is helped, compared to fourteen friends just having a fun day in the park who are left to drown. Where's the justice there?"

"Unpredictables don't help us. Why should they? What have we ever done to earn their respect and trust?" I asked.

"Well exactly," agreed Jim. "I think if they die in a petty squabble it's not our problem." He was very uptight about unpredictables. He didn't want anything to do with them.

"Unpredictables and hamsters are the same, they're greedy, selfish monsters," replied the Professor.

"Great, Professor, I at last agree with you about something," smiled Jim. "So Louis, why did the beast not stop at Bell-Sized Park like it did for me before?"

"I can't answer every question for you. Maybe the Bell-Sized spider's loose on the line, I dunno. Stop asking me stupid questions will you!"

The mechanical beast began squeaking and shuddered to a halt. It was a few yards from a new higher level and it gently chugged towards it. This though, was a horrible sight. It was one that sent an ice-cold shiver up and down our spines. You see, we'd arrived in the worst town ever imaginable…

HAMSTERED

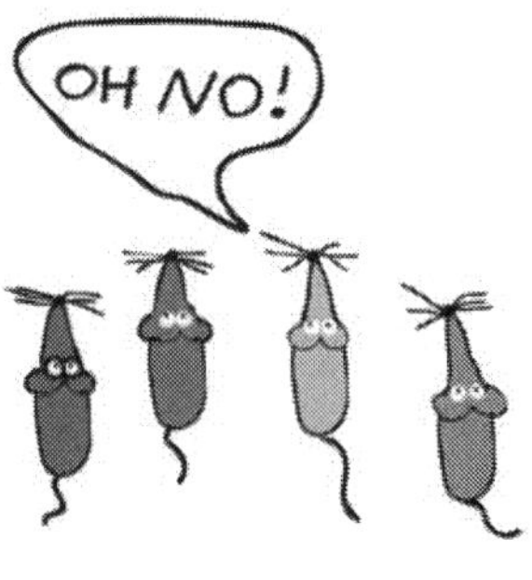

2. Hamstered

"Louis," sighed Jim. "Don't you think it may be a little bit more than a coincidence that Hamstered is similar to hamsters. Yet you told us that the hamsters come from a town called Kennington and that they are all Scottish."

"Are you calling me a liar?"

"No, I'm not saying that directly but, well, it looks promising."

"Hamstered, I believe is a town where a notorious gang have set up shop. They live by their wits. I didn't wanna come here as it's one of the scariest places in the world; we'll have to get ready for dangerous situations. Look! It was only due to bad fortune that we're here, it's not my fault!"

"So, you believe a gang live here. A dangerous gang. Do you reckon it's the gang that has kidnapped the 2nd heir to the throne of Jerboa?"

"Richard might be here somewhere, yes."

"It is written that you have to strike when the kettle's hot. Look, all of you, over there." We followed the pointed finger of Louis which took us in the direction of a grassy area named Hamstered Heath. On this heath we could see a mist, a cloud. Was this where our White Energy helper the Ssssylfia manifestation lived? Or was this a different kind of white mist?

Hang on… it looked more like the steam from a kettle. It is written that a notorious gang of hamsters have been described as major tea drinkers. They each store this tea in their own lockets that hang around their fluffy necks. They also have different, individual tea tastes.

"It is written that herbal tea is related to gerbil tea yet hamsters are not keen on milk. I never really understood this scroll, but if hamsters like tea without milk then maybe it becomes clearer and less clouded," suggested Louis.

"Well the tea would be less milky and darker," muttered Jim. "But say White Energy is milk related, so Dark Energy being, well, the opposite, may be a drink without milk. Do you think that's possible Max?"

"I don't think that's right at all," sighed the Professor.

"Nor me," I said. But Jim wasn't happy that his theory was ignored. He and Louis were at loggerheads again and the atmosphere between my friends was getting really bad. Max suggested we should leave them alone for a bit. Let their idle squabbling continue without our help. He gently grabbed my paw and we sneaked away to a large mound of grass about 30 yards behind our feuding friends. I wasn't totally happy about leaving the protection of Louis behind but Jim's attitude was getting worse by the minute and a fight between them looked on the cards. And in the blink of an eye, we were gone…

"So Louis what are we to do?" asked Jim. "I'm not amused with your funny plans. Are we to join our hamster foes? Slurp tea and munch upon a couple of biscuits and then slip in that we need this Richard character as he's the *ONE* we're looking for. Of course he might not really be the *ONE*, we might be wrong, but can we take him from you anyway."

"You don't have to be so sarcastic," groaned Louis. "Every mouse knows that hamsters can't refuse a challenge. All we've gotta do is challenge them to a game we can't lose. Then collect our prize, Richard."

"Yeah but say we do lose, what then?"

"Then we give them something that they want."

"Like what Louis?"

"Like a valley laced with more peanuts than imaginable. Like a mountain of the finest tea."

"So, how do we get that then? Will we just happen to stumble across it on the way to this heath? And anyway, what makes you think that these hamsters will succumb to a game? And what game have you in mind?"

"It is written that it's not what game you play but how you play the game."

"You've lost me?" sulked Jim.

"It's a mind thing see. If we can give the illusion of victory, even if we're struggling, someone or something will clinch our success."

"Like what?" quizzed Jim.

"Like a solution."

"You're mad!"

"No! I'm focused."

"He's mad isn't he Jane? Jane?" Jim looked towards where the place I had been standing with the Professor, but we were gone. His endless moaning had driven us away.

"They left," said Louis. He knew we'd gone and just neglected to tell Jim.

"What? Where are they?" complained Jim. He was frantically scurrying around. He sniffed trees, kicked tiny stones on the dirt track. He'd taste the air and tried to catch our scent. But all to no avail.

"They have headed down that concrete river towards the woods. Look!" Louis pointed to us on the horizon. We observed the paws pointed in our direction and we were about to wave back when we reached the brow of a mound and found ourselves cornered by the Collective.

"Look!" squeaked Jim. "Up there on the grassy knoll. Yes! I can see them. That's definitely them."

Jim could see us on the horizon, although the sun must have been blinding him slightly. He just seemed to wave back.

"Look! The Professor's waving, hello," he shouted.

"I do hope they stay put," said a concerned Louis. "What we don't want is to face these hamsters as a team of just two."

The Professor broke free temporarily and desperately tried to make a signal towards Jim and Louis before he was knocked down and taken off with me, deep into the woods. The Collective took us to a clearing near a large white house. It belonged to the dreaded chief hamster Ken Archdeacon. A hamster wearing a red locket taped our mouths up so we couldn't talk or squeak. We then overheard a master plan just completed by this gang. These hamsters, we heard, had been chosen for a big job. They were part of Ken's Collective alright, but not the usual breed of hamsters and nothing like the cute Collective that we had met in Mor's Den all those days ago. These were thugs. They were hardened hamsters with enormous muscles and shaven heads. We heard Ken calling them funny names, kind of nicknames I guess. Each one carried a locket around their neck and each one had a particular type of tea leaf variety inside it. These tea leaves were also used as their pretend names. It was odd that they liked tea as it didn't seem very Scottish. So maybe Louis was right as he did tell us once that not all hamsters were Scottish. Would it be that the Scottish ones are okay and these big, nasty looking ones were the real danger. What I did know was that myself and Max were gagged and tied up. That we'd deserted our colleagues at probably the most dangerous town we'd ever been too.

The new Collective were cleaner and sharper. I managed to wriggle my head free and noticed the name of the building in this heath area. It said: Kenwood House. Yes, it was starting to make sense. Ken Archdeacon, Kennington, Kenwood House. I wondered how many other places has he named himself after. He must be the main hamster and to have a house in Hamstered says a lot about his power and influence.

The new Collective were sitting in a circle and eating. The thing I think is funny about hamsters is their ability to eat and eat and eat. Their cheeks, through evolution, have grown pouches to store their food and these greedy rodents can now talk and eat at the same time. These giants were no ordinary run-of-the-mill hamsters. These six were the elite sewer rats of their species. The go-getters. It is written that nothing comes to those who wait; for if you wait, you'll die waiting.

Max was beginning to wriggle. He was belted on the head and knocked unconscious when we first arrived. I was worried that he was dead as the hamster dumped his body next to mine. I know that he does tend to squeak a lot when he's got a headache, but as he was gagged he'd just have to endure the pain, like me.

Although tied up we were positioned quite close and I thought it odd that we were allowed to hear their plans. It was horrible watching them and not being able to do anything. They all sat in their circle by a big lake. Ken Archdeacon was the only one standing. He had a kind of boyish grin on his face. I wondered if he had adopted this through his genes or it was something that became part of his nature.

PepperMint was the leader of this Collective. He was slightly green in colour and had rat-like camouflage skills. He had a mottled face with piercing dark eyes; and he was huge. He would be the one who'd authorise the others when on a job. I know this because as well as being in charge he was also cocky. He was running this team and he'd rub his team mates noses in it.

It is written in the Sacred Scrolls that the *ONE* will free and unite the rodent population. Louis says we need to find the *ONE* but what if Ken was the *ONE*? Could we then negotiate with this hamster? If only Louis were here, he'd know what to do. He is the one we need to defeat or befriend Ken. Wait a minute! Did I say he is the *ONE*? Is this *ONE* Ken or is it actually Louis or someone or something else?

PepperMint's second in command was slightly shorter but equally menacing. His name was DarJeeling. He was a sandy colour and had penetrating red eyes; he was very scary and very quiet. He'd oversee the others, check they were joining in rather than playing or fighting amongst themselves. Third in command was EarlGrey. He was, of course, grey, and at night he was almost invisible. He was quite a dashing looking hamster, although he didn't look half as attractive as Jim. Then the others CamoMile, RedBush and DaVid, these were the runners. They were used to sneak and slither and cheat to victory. RedBush looked a little small to be a hamster, he contained a few, dare I say it, gerbil qualities. CamoMile was good at controlling situations if things went wrong. He wouldn't panic. He was calm. The exception to the tea themed nicknames came in the shape of DaVid. He was the son of MacDrid. It was written that MacDrid was old and losing his touch and that he was a founding member of the Scottish Forefathers. He no longer walks and has to be carried and uses magnetic and electrical methods to communicate. It was Ken's idea that DaVid be around for this heist. After all, when the time comes and MacDrid dies, DaVid will become one of the Lower London Controllers. Oh no! Maybe he is the *ONE*? He was learning the trade through work experience under the watchful eyes of his uncle Ken.

The Collective Hamsters

The numbers specify order of quality control

PepperMint	***No.1***
DarJeeling	***No.2***
EarlGrey	***No.3***
CamoMile	***No.4***
RedBush	***No.5***
DaVid	***No.6***

Ken spoke of a palace filled with peanuts and tea and that would be their next job. He then thanked them for a successful mission but had a couple of complaints. I guess some hamsters are never happy, they're always picking at something. He didn't seem to mention Richard at all, at least I didn't hear that he did.

"PepperMint, your command was critical. You all arrived at Ally Pally at 02:00. There was a woofer there, correct. Now, you had twelve minutes and thirty seconds to distract it. I suggested that you and RedBush, CamoMile and DaVid taunt this beast, then run away making it chase you. Now, I was watching from the brow of the knoll and when RedBush ran out of energy, you were slow, DaVid, at giving the signal to CamoMile, but he was alert enough to take your place. You others were fine, bang on. This meant you all had to run over three minutes and ten seconds each. I should have said prepare to run for four minutes as it would have made you fitter. You see, these stupid unpredictables didn't notice that this woofer was gone for nearly thirteen minutes, so in hindsight I think we were a tad lucky. We got Crazy's magnetic platform so that's all that counts. In a separate Smash-n-Grab mission it was then your turn DarJeeling and EarlGrey. You two had to sneak in and fetch the prize Rodent Key which was to be found hidden in the fourteenth book in the Great Library marked with that Pi symbol. You avoided conflict with the scratcher too, well done. It's great that you got it, but time was tight. Next time be sharper okay! What I'm saying to you today must not go outside this group. I don't want you discussing the plan in front of those two mice you captured earlier, one slip up and it could cost us dear."

Ken then waved towards a large crow. It was carrying a large basket in its claws. It swooped down and there, in the basket, was a great hoard of pies. The Collective took no time in munching there way through them. The exception was RedBush, he wasn't interested. He definitely looked shifty and odd that this hamster wasn't hungry and in a flash, he was gone.

I assume Ken didn't notice that RedBush had placed myself and Max within audible range of his babbling. Why did RedBush do this? Surely he was a clever enough hamster not to make simple errors, unless of course he was a spy. After all he was the one who was fractionally smaller. There I go again when I'm thinking; I'm saying to myself he's the *ONE*.

Meanwhile Louis and Jim were still searching for us. "Jim, look here." Louis pointed to the Professor's sack of inventions lying on the ground.

"I don't like the look of this, there's no way he'd leave those behind unless he's trying to tell us something," replied Jim.

"Yeah, I agree. He's probably been dragged off somewhere. Look! On the ground over there, it looks as though there's been a scuffle...."

"Over here Louis..." Jim had found something in the bushes. "It looks like a crimson scarf. Why is there a crimson scarf in the bushes? Unless… yes! Crimson Pigs is here somewhere, but where? Hang on, there's also some kind of key with an inscription on it. It says: *The Rodent Key*. I reckon he must have dropped it. But where is he now? How come he hasn't come back for it? Why hasn't he told us he is here and on our side?"

"Jim, there's paw prints and a trail leading into the woods, as though someone has dragged something along the ground. Let's follow it." The two of them headed towards where we were. Jim was a good tracker. He used to study shapes in the ground for fun. I remember him telling me once that it's the shape and weight of certain things that leads to their downfall. By working out their meaning he can find a weakness and exploit it. Hamsters have been known throughout the generations as being dreadful spellers. Is this the way we'd deal with these hamsters

"I can see them Louis! Look! There they are over there," whispered Jim. He pointed in our direction. I could see them both but as I was still gagged and tied up I could do nothing about it. "How are we gonna get them out of this fix?"

"Tricky?" said Louis. "Err, let's see if we can get their attention, but whatever you do don't fall in the lake or the hamsters will see us..."

I watched as my friends crawled towards us, then disappeared. Where were they?

"Professor! Pssst! Professor, Jane.....over here." I could hear voices behind me somewhere. I then noticed a reflection in the lake and I saw Louis' fluffy face. He must have followed us here, but I couldn't talk because of the gag in my mouth. I wondered if Louis had a clear view of all these hamsters. Surely if they saw him he'd be a goner. Then I saw Jim's reflection, he whispered something in Louis' ear but I couldn't make it out. I wonder what he said…

3. Game of Words

I watched as Jim displayed signs of either enormous bravery or unrivalled stupidity. He scampered right up to the main hamster, Ken Archdeacon. He was mumbling a little, but I believe he was trying to strike up some kind of deal.

"Hi Mr Hamster. My name's Jim Amadeus Jerbil and I know what you're thinking Mr Hamster, but cast that from your mind. How would you like to challenge me to a game of Words?"

"Words! Ha! Ha!" Ken laughed. We are trying to eat but I'm sure we can play Words and eat too. The rest of the Collective became agitated and just stared at Jim. They couldn't believe the guts of this mouse.

"I want Richard, 2nd heir to the throne of Jerboa as my prize when I win," said Jim.

"If you win," smirked Ken.

"The rules are two verses two. i.e. two mice against two hamsters. Are you game?"

"Yes! Ha! Ha! But pray tell, what do I get if I win?"

"You get the Rodent Key?" grinned Jim. He was smiling at Ken but I was sure it was a nervous grin.

"What! You have the key! But how?"

"Yes Ken, I have the key."

"But how?…" Ken became annoyed and stared at his Collective. I then saw EarlGrey scamper to Ken and whisper in his ear, alas I couldn't hear the conversation, but it seemed to cheer Ken up no end. "My number one and two will play for me. Who's playing for you?"

Jim pointed towards the Professor, "Release that mouse there please. I'm number one and he's my number two; my second."

"So mouse, do you have the game with you?" Ken asked.

"Yes." Jim reached into the Professor's sack of inventions and pulled out the pre-made game. He then pulled out the universal edition of Rodent's first dictionary.

Ken pulled his gang to one side and started whispering again. He then changed direction and pointed at me and Professor, “Get that mouse one of you!” He turned his glare to CamoMile who nonchalantly walked over, untied the Professor and brought him over. “Ha! Great! Are you ready mice? Let the game commence.”

After EarlGrey left with the Professor, Louis rescued me. It was bizarre watching them playing that game. It was quite a crisp day. It felt cold when I was bound and gagged, but now I was free and in the bushes with Louis, sheltered from the wind.

Jim was quite good at Words. We noticed he was winning easily. It came as a shock that he didn't want Louis to play. Louis knows more words than any mouse I've ever known. It was pleasant for us to laze on the grass. It was just a nice, enjoyably, relaxing wait. They hadn't noticed I’d been rescued as they were more interested in the game, the Rodent Key, but mainly the pies.

“Where do you think Richard is?” I asked Louis.

“He might be tied up in Ken’s White House, or maybe on that floating raft over there,” he said, pointing towards a piece of awning covering a floating thing that was drifting slowly in the lake.

“What makes you think he's over there?” I asked.

“Well, I heard strange noises coming from it when I swam across to help you.”

"Wait! Look over there!" I squealed. The hamster known as RedBush was picking Jim's pocket. We watched him as he plucked the Rodent Key from it and hid it in his own coat. He then grabbed the Professor's sack of inventions. The next thing we knew we saw RedBush scampering back towards the station. Louis and myself followed in hot pursuit.

"Quickly Jane, we can't let him have them."

After about five minutes of intense scampering a thought struck me. What would happen to Jim and the Professor if we left them there with those horrid hamsters? I asked Louis, "Okay! Okay, but what about our friends? We can't leave them there, surely."

"Err, okay. You follow that hamster and I'll try and get Jim and the Professor back." And off he went.

He left me to fulfil his task. He snubbed me. I scampered after RedBush thinking of what would happen if he turned towards me. I was so scared and yet I was even more scared for my friends who were playing Words with possibly the nastiest hamster gang in history. This made me kind of hesitant and I remember looking back, skidding on the white frosty ground and seeing Louis just about to reveal himself to Ken when…

CLUNK! I must have knocked myself out…

Due to my injury I felt unwell and dopey. The white flakes of Mor's Den were here too. They fell from the sky and dissolved on my furry body. But I quite liked them this time. They were soothing. I crawled on my own, a few yards, to a big oak tree and crept inside. I lay on the ground amongst the icy bark crystals and feel asleep. In Louis' version of events (as I was told them later) he detailed my foolishness and my accident prone nature. Louis said that I'd run straight into a tree. He told me that it is written that if you don't watch where you're going sometimes it can be very painful. I took this to be a very truthful scroll as I was bleeding and I had an awful headache.

Louis' Story

Back at the game Jim and Max were doing very well.

The Collective of brutish hamsters were intimidating, but they weren't the most intelligent rodents in the woods. They were obviously good at being nasty or plotting things, but playing Words was definitely their Achilles heel.

"Look, that's not a word, you can't have that!" moaned Jim. He was arguing with a hamster maybe three times bigger than him. Yet because of the strangeness of the game, it seemed the logical thing to do.

"M-I-C-E-R is a word," explained DarJeeling. "It means a scratcher that likes chasing mice." DarJeeling looked annoyed. He turned towards Ken for inspiration but Ken just laughed at him.

"No! I'd have to agree with Jim. Look I'll challenge that," replied the Professor. He was confident in Jim's ability to see a fault with these hamsters. He was scared of them for sure, but happy that Jim was the main rival for success.

"But when you find it's in there you'll lose a go," groaned PepperMint. He had his hands on his hips and was continually eating throughout the whole game.

"No! That's not the rules," moaned Jim. "In the rules it specifies that I can challenge any word I want. If I wanted I could challenge the word *Hamster*, but I know that's in there and is described as a fat mouse that can't stop eating."

"Are you calling me fat?" moaned PepperMint. He put the large pie he was about to take a bite out of on the floor next to him and seemed sad.

"Well you are, look at you," said the Professor. He leaned over to PepperMint and poked him in the tummy.

"Ow! Look stop poking me and get on with the game. So what does it say in the Rodent dictionary?"

"It's not there," smirked the Professor. Ha! You were probably thinking of M-O-U-S-E-R. Ha! Ha!"

"Right, it's my go I think, as you miss a go," grinned Jim. "Err… oh goody and guess what? I've got a seven letter word! It's G-I-G-G-L-E-S. Let's see. 19 points for the letters, that second G's on a bonus square giving me a extra 10 points and 100 points for getting rid of all my letters, that's 129 for me and better than that I'm out. I've won. Superb!"

"Well done Jim, you're the first mouse I've known to score over 350!" smiled Max. "My previous best was 10 less. Having said that, when I got my top score we weren't playing useless hamsters."

"Ken, you're an honourable rodent. We hereby claim our prize, Richard," squeaked Jim. He was so full of glee. He was rubbing his paws together and jumping up and down with joy.

"Well that's unfortunate because he's not here," gloated Ken. "He's in a safe place far, far away. Your only hope for him is to find the bottle."

"The bottle contains magical Dark Matter juices," replied CamoMile.

"Shhh! Don't tell the fools. Ha! Ha!" muttered DaVid.

"Well at least we've got the Rodent Key," answered Jim. He dipped his hand in his pocket but it was gone. "Where is it? But I had it?" He was frantically looking around and then stared back at Ken. "Was it you who took it from me?"

"You're not so cocky now are you mouse? My good friend RedBush has got it. He's hiding on that raft. RedBush! Hey! RedBush! You can come out now?" But he did not appear. "Come on RedBush, the coast is clear." Still the raft stayed motionless. Then I (Louis) came out of hiding and trotted towards my confused friends and the hamsters.

"RedBush is long gone," I sighed.

"And who are you?" asked a confused Ken. "Another little mouse who knows what exactly?"

And that was that. Another confusing journey ended with a more confusing end, or was it the end. These hamsters were at least talking, they weren't fighting, eating or changing us into pecan nuts yet so maybe we as rodents shared a common goal…

4. The Crimson Connection

Louis' Story continued…

I was sure more than ever that the Rodent Key was vital to discovering and fulfilling our destinies, but with these hamsters after it too, life was getting tougher by the day.

Ken wasn't happy about seeing me and repeated his question, "Who are you mouse?"

"I'm Louis the Furred. 3rd in line to the throne of Jerboa. I was once 13th in line but your nasty brother has killed most of my older brothers. Richard is 2nd in line, he is my brother and I want to see him again. But, what's more concerning is that we both have a major problem. You see, I believe RedBush wasn't really RedBush. Did you not think he looked a little small for a hamster? If you're saying Richard is somewhere else then I'm saying so is RedBush. As a hunch I reckon that the real RedBush is, as you have said, on that raft, but he's not hiding, he's gagged. I can say this as I've heard noises on it. I can also tell you that the impostor RedBush is actually the legendary Crimson Pigs. A crossbred gerbil and the one we need. Listen to me carefully hamster, my colleague Jane is following him."

Ken and some of the Collective went to the edge of the lake and pulled a rope and tugged the raft to the bank. They removed the awning and what I'd expected was true, there amongst the soggy ropes was a gagged, unhappy and very hungry hamster.

"One of you untie your colleague!"

I watched as PepperMint helped the shaken hamster to his feet and fed him some pie that he stored in his cheeks. Ken then took me to one side and said, "So you say you've got someone following him?"

"Yes, Jane. She's one of my team and is on his trail."

"Number one and number two you go with these mice and find Crimson Pigs and I don't want any slip ups."

"Okay boss," they replied in unison.

We set off as a group. It was funny in a way to be scampering along with two giant hamsters as chaperones. Or was it that they were Hit-mice? Either way we were a team although this was to be short lived. We ran towards a grassy knoll and saw three intimidating black and white scratchers watching us in the undergrowth. Jim then shrieked as he pointed to about five or six round faces in the trees above. The Collective hamsters were not afraid and sheltered us from these stalking beasts that lurked in the bushes and branches. On the horizon we saw what looked like Jane. But she was bleeding and whining and trying to alert us her to position. It was awful being a vulnerable mouse in an unfamiliar place. We scampered towards her. I stroked her fluffy face and she smiled. This smile then turned to panic as she saw the giant PepperMint and nasty DarJeeling hamsters with her friends. She squeaked but calmed down after I told her they were on our side. She sighed and took a long breath, we hugged and were friends again. Jim and the Professor were happy to see her alive too, but unhappy at the new and challenging world that we had found.

Jane's Story

So that was Louis' story as he told it to me. Next he asked me, "Jane, what's happened, why are you still here?" He looked upset and embarrassed at my failing as a tracker.

"Oh, I hit my head," I cried.

"Great!.....Unreliable mice!" cursed PepperMint. "We'll go back and tell Ken and if you want this Richard, you'd better find us the Rodent Key. Then we'll have do a meet and do a trade. Do you know the church owned by the king?"

"No?" replied Louis.

"Well you better find out where it is, we'll give you one week. Meet us in the middle at noon if you wanna see Richard alive. Ha! Ha!" chuckled the hamsters and then, like magic, they were gone.

"Superb!" Jim howled sarcastically. "We're hunting for Richard, Crimson Pigs a crossbred gerbil and now we've got a deadline with the reservoir hamsters next week regarding the Rodent Key! There's a bottle of magical Dark Matter juice to find although we don't know what that is either. What else? Oh yeah, and not forgetting of course we've somehow gotta find the *ONE* to help us understand this Dark Energy! Also we may have accidentally found White Energy but then again maybe it wasn't... I... I...I need a sit down."

"We need to find my stepbrother too," groaned Max.

"Oh yeah, that too," huffed Jim. He sat on the grass by the edge of the Heath and looked depressed. He then said, "I reckon we should try and find Max's stepbrother Paul in Bell-Sized Park next. At least we know he's there because I dropped him there myself. Having said that, maybe he been moved or taken elsewhere and this will be another wild goose chase."

"Jim, moaning about what we've gotta do isn't gonna get it done is it?" argued Louis.

"I suppose not," he replied.

"Well then."

"Well then what Louis? Well then what?"

"Well then let's start at the beginning and retrace our steps."

"What? Go all the way back to Clapham shops? I'm not going back there!" squeaked Jim. "Let's find Paul."

"Wait! Hang on! Where's my sack of inventions?" asked Max.

"Oh, we saw that Crimson take it, you know the one that's got the Rodent Key," I replied.

"And pray tell, where's he gone to?" asked Max.

"I heard him mutter something about a white round face?" I answered. "I don't know where that is though."

"So where's that Jane?" asked Louis.

"I just told you, I'm not sure. We could ask the Bell-Sized spider. It's only a suggestion, as we've gotta go there anyway to find Paul."

"Yeah, let's head for Bell-Sized Park then," said Louis. We scampered back to the station area. A mechanical beast came straight away and we climbed onto the bumper. Louis looked like he was expecting to see the Ssssylfia but it didn't appear. We rushed off into the blackness and within a minute we had arrived at the Bell-Sized Park's higher level. Jim took the lead as he'd been there before. We took a left out of the station entrance and into the park…

5. Bell-Sized Park Hides Secrets

"It's up here somewhere, the bell, I've seen it," squeaked Jim.

"Oh yes! Nice, soft, lush grass. I'm just gonna stretch my legs," mumbled the Professor and off he scampered with Jim in hot pursuit.

"Wait for me! I'm coming with you!" Jim turned back towards me and shouted, "are you coming too, Jane?"

"No it's okay, I'll stay with Louis."

"Don't do anything stupid," screamed Louis. "Just get that pecan and come back to the station. If you can't find it then don't worry because I'll ask the Bell-Sized spider later after its eaten." But, as they'd already run far away into the distance, I wasn't sure that they'd heard him. Louis looked at me in disbelief. He said, "Well Jane. I think they understood but I'm not sure. I reckon we should sit here and wait for them to come back then, I suppose. But hide yourself as I don't want us to be a scratchers' or round faces' meal tonight."

Louis and I sat on the grass. He reckoned that the others wouldn't find Paul anywhere. He'd already given up hope of their success. He wasn't the kind of mouse who gave responsibility to others normally. He really wasn't in a happy mood anymore. I suppose he was just being himself and allowing his friends the freedom to explore. But I guess he knew, when it came to the crunch, that dangers and problematic situations would ensue if they failed in their task.

"If we wait till dusk this spider should be full and may be helpful," Louis suggested.

"Are we really going to speak to a spider that eats mice… like us… is that wise?" I asked. I was confused by Louis' plan. You see, I'd never spoken to a spider before, but Louis said he had.

"I remember in the shop in Clapham when an unpredictable came in with some very nasty looking hairy spiders. They were apparently from South America, from Brazil I think," said Louis. He was lying on the slightly worn grassy patch with his paws and arms tucked behind his head. He seemed very relaxed for someone who would be risking his life for maybe nothing.

Louis told me he got on quite well with a spider called Luciano who lived in our Clapham shop. He said Luciano wasn't a caged or captured beast, he was free. He'd scavenge for food like little insects, woodworms and moths. Louis told me this male spider used to talk of death quite a lot. He'd say how Luciano used to talk about how many animals that he'd attacked and killed and consumed.

"Do you remember Luciano?" asked Louis.

"I'm not sure I was born then," I answered.

"He was the hairiest animal I've ever seen! Mice are furry but he was really hairy. Scratchers are furry but woofers are hairy, funny that isn't it? Anyway, Luciano wasn't really that big, but had eight eyes and they all used to point in different directions."

"You're scaring me," I squeaked.

"Did you know that some spiders have eyes at the back of their heads? It is written that the Bell-Sized spider has two faces. So maybe she too will see us coming even when not looking." Louis stood up and stared at me. "This is not necessarily a good thing, Jane. It is written that the most dangerous creature is the one that's two-faced. Have you ever met anyone like that?"

"Yes! You," I replied. I started to cry. I knew I'd upset him. But I had to tell him as he had upset me before when he'd shown me his true colours. I was so unhappy. I was annoyed with Jim and the Professor but Louis was our leader and he had the responsibility to be honest and trustworthy.

"That's not very nice." He turned away from me and scampered to the centre of a flower bed. He said, "There's a way of talking to hungry spiders. Humouring them doesn't work. I must possess courage, and this is what Luciano said I should do. If a spider is faced by an animal that isn't afraid, he may earn their respect and may live. I'm scared Jane, but I must go alone to see this spider, to understand it's wisdom. I must wait for him to finish his last meal. The ghost, the Ssssylfia, said this in her vision, or disaster will strike and I'll be wrapped and eaten too." And with that he hugged me, wiped the tears from my eyes and left.

"Bye Louis. I love you… " I watched as he headed alone up the large grassy knoll. Was this the last I'd see of him? Maybe Jim was right and I should have gone with them, at least they were safe.

I was confused because I thought we were a team and yet this group was always breaking up. I wasn't happy that Jim and Max had deserted us, but I was more unhappy at the prospect of living the rest of my days alone and under the watchful eyes of vicious hungry creatures that lurk in the shadows.

I turned away from Louis and hid myself again under a small, flimsy bag, which I think unpredictables call a crisp packet. It was a good choice. The insulation of the foil wrapping against my furry body created a vacuum of warmth. I was small enough to hide fully underneath it and I was feeling relatively happier than before until I thought I heard someone crying…

"Jane! Over here." I could hear the faint cries of somebody calling my name. I poked my head out and sniffed the air. It was becoming cold and my breath turned into a white mist. Was this another form of White Energy? Did it matter? I was confused. Then suddenly, the crying seemed to get louder as the sky turned darker and the echoing voice called out my name again "Jane! Over here… " I looked all around but I saw no one. Where was this voice coming from?

Then suddenly a silhouetted shape appeared in the distance. I squinted slightly and raised my right paw over my eyebrows to stop the overpowering light from blinding me. Then I could just about recognise the outline of my friend, Max. It looked as though he was standing by a large crater, but where was Jim? Behind Max there was a strong, fierce light, which seemed to flicker, and buzzy moths appeared from nowhere and dive-bombed into his face.

I scurried over. "What is it Max? What?"

"It's Jim," he said. He was pointing towards a dark cavern and I saw tears in his eyes. "Jim's fallen down that chasm... can you see him?"

"Yeah, just about," I said. I reached towards Jim but he seemed complacent. Then that feeling of déjà vu struck me. I'd seen that face before. He had that dream-like expression on his face, the same one he'd had at Cam's Den when he was dreaming of strawberries. I asked him, "Are you okay?"

"Yeah, I think so," he echoed back. "I've fallen in this hole and it's full of white powder and loads of different types of nuts."

"That's a relief," I sighed. "I can see Max up here but he's standing in front of a bright light."

"Are you coming down Jane?" Jim asked.

"Maybe in a moment. I just need to ask Max something. Err, what's that light Professor?"

"It's coming from one of those ear-ringed unpredictables' machines," he replied.

"So why's he left it there?" I asked.

"Jane, how do you expect me to know?"

"Well is it relevant?"

"Yes very."

"Why?"

"Because without him it would be pitch black here. Maybe it's an omen," Max answered.

"What's an omen?"

"It's similar to the Ssssylfia. It's a sign. A bizarre happening. I believe the unpredictable machine is here for a reason. It came to help us. I think this omen is Dark Energy and the Ssssylfia is White Energy."

Out of nowhere Louis appeared, but as usual these days he didn't seem very happy. "What's going on?"

"Oh Jim's stuck down that hole," I said pointing. "and we're being blinded by Dark Energy."

"That's not Dark Energy!" Louis stood with his paws on his hips and looked distraught. "Have you learnt nothing? Look…. I've spoken to the spider and she said that all the pecans were taken to a special place. Some are used as pretend eggs for a white round face. This round face is dangerous and lives on a white farm near here."

"Hey! Hey! Down here Louis," screamed Jim. Louis babbling and moaning had alerted Jim, who was persistent in his desire to get us all down there with him. "Come on! Jump down, there's a tunnel down here too and lots of white powder. Come on! All of you come down."

Louis sighed and we all jumped down. Where Jim was standing amongst the white powder we saw a Max-Lantern.

"Someone's been using my inventions," moaned the Professor.

"That will be that *tea-leaf*, what's-his-name? RedBush!" I squeaked.

"Crimson Pigs you mean," groaned Louis. "The crossbred gerbil who loves to steal things. Look, there's a trail of red-coloured tea leaves going down that passage way there." He pointed towards the trail of leaves. We followed it and arrived at a cave. Inside we could see Crimson Pigs. He was trying to open a pecan with a set of Max-Nutcrackers. Louis crept up on him. "Crimson! we meet again."

"Argh! You surprised me. Look I can explain. The round face made me do it. Look at him up there. He's asleep now but if he wakes we'll be eaten for sure." Crimson pointed to a sleeping, big-eyed creature. "He's North American. You see how he's got a speckled plumage. He feeds on nuts. If he wakes before I find the *ONE* it will be a disaster."

"What are you really up to Crimson? I remember months ago when you were a good gerbil, now you're nothing but a no good thief. You stole the Rodent Key from Jim and the Professor's sack of inventions, why?"

"You can't let Ken and his Collective have the key you know. If he lets his brother Andrew use it again then all the rodents in London will become nuts, like these." He pointed, and the worrying image created by his words came to light. Yes, he was trying to crack a pecan nut open, but as our eyes adjusted to the darkness we found we were standing in a cave filled with an assortment of hundreds upon hundreds of nuts.

"Oh my, there's so many," said Louis.

"Also, that sack of inventions is mine. I mislaid it in Clapham. I went back for it but it was gone. The reason I'm here is I need to find the *ONE*. I know it's in one of these nuts somewhere it just takes a lot of finding."

"Professor, I thought the inventions were yours?" quizzed Louis. He wasn't very happy with Max's lying.

"They are mine, he's the one that's lying," replied the Professor sadly.

"So what is this *ONE* and why do you need the Rodent Key?" asked Louis. For the first time for ages it wasn't just me that didn't know what was happening. Louis, our leader, was confused too. What made this worse was that Crimson wasn't a nice rodent, he was a rude and disrespectful crossbreed and that made the situation awkward.

"Look, no offence," said Crimson, "but I can't tell you that. I dunno who you are. You might be working with the reservoir hamsters. I saw you lot myself playing Words with them. I can't believe they agreed to play you, they must be mad, mustn't they?"

"Why can't you tell us about the *ONE* or that Rodent Key?" Louis asked again.

"Look, you help me find, err, how can I say this without......err, do any of you know the crossbreed Paul? We were in Andrew's lair in the end-of-the-tracks town Mor's Den. Anyway he knows about the *ONE*... but without his knowledge, err... well, this is a secret, so don't go babbling it around and don't tell hamsters... but... "

"Well spit it out Crimson you're mumbling," complained Jim.

"He's the *ONE* you seek," said Crimson.

"Who is? Paul?" asked Louis.

"Well, he is one of the *ONES* you seek."

"So you're saying he's the *ONE* but there's more than one *ONE*! But we had him, damn!" Louis sulked on the ground.

"Paul, my stepbrother is the *ONE*? Wow! See I told you Louis, that he's not the kind of mouse to run away for no reason."

"Things are really beginning to make sense at last," sighed Louis.

"I disagree. Nothing makes senses and I'm totally confused," moaned Jim. He looked at me and we both had blank expressions on our fluffy faces. What was going on here?

"Look, not total sense just a little more sense," growled Louis. "I remember when Paul used to speak of him being created for a purpose. I used to say to him that the only reason why he was born was to make other mice look superior. How wrong was I?"

"Louis please don't get too carried away. I've just had a thought. It might be a different Paul," I said.

"I'd agree with that. Paul was small," the Professor mentioned. "And this pecan that Crimson is trying to crack open with my invention is enormous."

"Listen mouse, it's my invention!" moaned Crimson. "And Paul may have been small before but as the pressure grows on the shell, inside he is swelling, thus making the shell bigger."

"Then maybe he is the *ONE*!" I squeaked. Crimson squeezed the giant pecan he thought was Paul into his coat and carried on attempting to crack open other small nuts that he had rescued from the round face's nest.

"Look, up there!" Louis pointed to the white round face, it was awake and watching us. It looked like it was laughing at our small pathetic bodies and our blistered feet. It seemed to stare at Jim the most…

6. Chalky Farm

The round face looked like it was worshipping Jim. It was like it knew him. It flew down from its nest and crouched in front of Jim and then spoke to him… "I am your master! Wooo! Wooo! You are my *ONE*! Wooo! Wooo!"

"What's going on?" Louis asked Crimson.

"It seems the round face believes Jim is the *ONE*. Anything that Jim wishes the round face will obey. It is written that a mysterious round face grants three wishes to the *ONE*."

"Master hey… and the *ONE*! Cool," chirped Jim. "Err, white round face can you bring me a whole load of fresh warm peanuts and nice juicy drink please."

"Your wish is my command." The round face flew high into the air and within seconds swooped down giving Jim everything he wanted.

Jim stuffed a large paw full of peanuts into his mouth and just as he was about to taste his magic drink Crimson stopped him "Wait! Don't drink that! It looks as though it has come from the Sacred Well. If you drink it you'll be turned into a pecan for sure."

But it was too late, both him and the Professor guzzled down the magic juice and within seconds both of them turned into pecans.

"No! It can't be. Jim! Professor!" I yelled, but it was no good. There was a slight crack in the side of Jim's shell, we could see only the whites of his eyes. He was compacted like sardines in a tin. He wriggled around inside until his whiskers stuck out, it was awful.

"Crimson, why did this happen? Is there a way we can free them? Will the Max-Nutcrackers work?" screamed Louis.

"My nutcrackers! Not Max-Nutcrackers! And they will only work on small rodents. Your colleague, that spectacled mouse, has grabbed my sack of inventions and is trapped tightly too. As for Jim well, he's a bit podgy so if we tried to crack him out he'll surely be crushed and will die. There is a way though. I have the Rodent Key and this opens the lock to a safe in a scientist's home. He has supposedly invented a magical DM liquid that can change pecans back into rodents. It is written that there is a place where every rodent may meet a crushing defeat. If we go there we have a chance."

"So let's go then, what are we waiting for?" I argued.

"Look mouse, I need to find Paul, don't you see? Your friends were foolish whereas I wasn't."

"But Crimson," squeaked Louis. "Myself and Jane will hunt high and low for Paul, but I feel we need to help our comrades Jim and Max, without them there is no point in going on."

"I cannot neglect my mission to find Paul. And anyway we'll need some inspiration as we don't know where to look."

"But Crimson, we have the power of our souls in control. Come, let's go this way." Louis led the way followed by me and Crimson. The round face sat and giggled to itself. It was the first time that the Sacred Scrolls had let us down. But wait! The Sacred Scrolls only work for those who have faith, for faith is part of the magic in everything we do. Jim didn't believe in them, therefore he was unfortunate. For the first time in our lives we'd seen Jim unlucky. That was truly odd. Louis led us to a shimmering opening. How did he know it was there? It was very dark and suddenly there was a flash of light, it was a spark from a beast. Louis had somehow led us to another higher level. This place was called Chalky Farm. Everything was coming together nicely.

"That's bizarre." Crimson was shocked that we'd stumbled across this area.

"Yes Crimson, this kind of thing happens to us quite often. Have you heard of the Ssssylfia?" Louis asked.

"I've heard of it but never seen it."

"Well I believe that today is going to be a more bizarre day for you, as today we have so many complicated problems and yet so few answers. Look and be patient."

We stood there confused, tired and upset. Crimson was holding a large swollen pecan which he thought was Paul. I was holding the Professor, also squashed inside a pecan shell. And

Louis had Jim (the pecan) in his arms. There was so much to do and so little time it was awful.

We stood on the higher level at Chalky Farm and watched as a mechanical beast disappeared down one of its tunnels and almost like clockwork the Ssssylfia emerged again with another riddle:

THE TASTE CAN BE DECEIVING
THE REACTION CAN BE REVEALING
BELGIUM MAYBE THE DOWNFALL
WHEN YOU MEET
YOUR WATERLOO

"I guess it means we head for WaterLoo then. That's not too far away is it Louis?" I asked. I knew our content of things to sort out was growing but getting our friends back, that was top of the list.

"Is that the Ssssylfia? I've never seen it before? And to think it may be another kind of White Energy, that's interesting," said Crimson.

"Look, I'm pretty sure the Ssssylfia is not White Energy. But we have to be a little worried here," answered Louis. "I believe we can't ignore what the ghost is saying. I believe one of us will meet something called Belgium at this WaterLoo place."

"Belgium is a country, so your previous remark made no sense," smirked Crimson.

"Sorry," Louis mumbled.

We waited together on the higher level. Another mechanical beast appeared from the blackness and we climbed on board the rear bumper. I hoped the magical Dark Matter juice the Collective spoke of could help our friends because I missed them. Yet my mind was occupied by thoughts far worse that this. The Collective had also threatened us in Hamstered. We needed to find a king's church at a place we had never heard of. Or was it Jim who was this king and would this place be connected to the throne of Jerboa?

I knew our only hope for our trapped friends was to steal the Rodent Key off Crimson Pigs, the crossbreed who was beginning to look like an ally rather than an enemy.

I sat at the edge of the bumper on my own and felt sad. I wondered whether I should have stayed with Eon, those rats and that scratcher Grimley in High Gate. I was sure now that whatever lay ahead it was to be more dangerous and more confusing than anything imaginable…

Dark Energy Visions

As Volume Two ends, the thoughts of our tasks were beginning to stack up. Louis and I were the only ones left standing after our escape from Clapham all those days ago. Yes Jim and Max were with us but trapped in the form of pecans, so awkward to carry. Crimson Pigs has emerged on the scene as our inspiration. A crossbreed that duped Ken Archdeacon and the Collective, who stole the Rodent Key from them and, although small is aggressive. He had joined forces with us but he didn't seem that trustworthy. As for Max's stepbrother Paul, his whereabouts may well have been in the pecan that Crimson was carrying, but Louis and I weren't convinced. I had learnt that Louis thinks Richard who is the 2nd in line to the throne of Jerboa, is also his brother and amazingly, he may well be the *ONE* we seek instead. Ironically, Jim has now emerged as a possible king. Is he the rightful heir to this throne? The white round face from Chalky Farm thinks Jim is its master but this dangerous creature also thinks that Jim, my friend, may be the *ONE* too. What was more confusing was that Crimson believes there is more than one *ONE*. Our scarlet ally believes that Paul is part of the rodent destiny and hides an answer to our dreams, but not the full answer.

Our new goal was set: to travel on the mechanical beast to WaterLoo, a place where, it said, *ONE* may die. Is *ONE* anyone of us? Is this the *ONE* that dies or a different *ONE*?

We needed more inspiration. And then, uncharacteristically and out of nowhere, the Ssssylfia appeared.

DARK ENERGY
WILL BECOME
VISIBLE WHEN
YOUR FRIENDS
BECOME INVISIBLE

"I don't understand Louis?" I squeaked. I am confused and scared.

"I don't understand either," said Crimson. He was totally dumbfounded by the second vision by a creation that he had only heard about in the Sacred Scrolls or in legends from the murky past. For him to be one of the few rodents to see and receive riddles made him even worse as a traveling companion. And he really started to bug Louis.

The Ssssylfia vanished and a shimmering picture appeared above the tracks instead, lit only by the sparks of the beast, as it raced through the blackness on route to WaterLoo. It was a vision of a stunning shimmering wall. There were black splatters of mud on this wall and then something truly bizarre happened. I don't know if the white face was close or it was a trick of the light, but we saw something very odd. At the corner of the wall we saw Jim standing and talking to the Bell-Sized spider. He was in Bell-Sized Park again. How could this be? Are we to go back on ourselves again to retrace our steps looking for something in a town that we had thought had no real significance?

Jim suggested earlier that Dark Energy was a force-field wall in Bell-Sized Park, but we ignored his babbling. Had he really found Dark Energy? If this wall was it, why was it not dark? This bizarre shimmering wall then revealed Jim as two creatures. On one side he was the fluffy mouse we know and love, yet on the other he was manifested as an unpredictable. He was slightly balding and had medals as if he was once a great warrior. I then cringed as I saw myself appear, at first as a mouse but then I changed into an unpredictable princess. Louis appeared to be crawling along the ground on his belly, then he too changed, but not into an unpredictable like me or Jim, but into an alligator. Finally, our attention turned to Max, and his shimmering reflection became a large smiling crocodile. It was as if all of Jim's exaggerated stories had come true. It scared me. Well, it scared all of us…

Crimson was upset by this vision as there was no image of him. Was it him that the Ssssylfia predicted would die at WaterLoo?

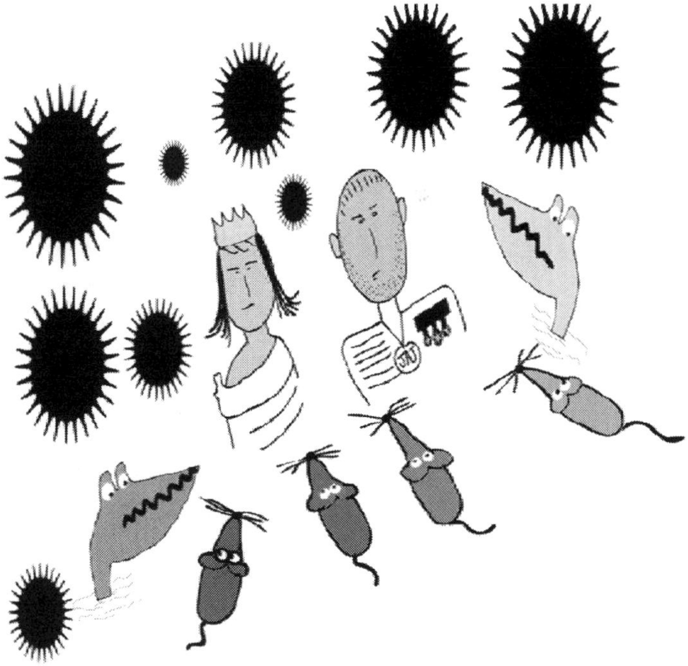

Louis was confused, well, we all were. Our leader just didn't have anything to say. We sat there on the bumper staring into the blackness and hoped it was all a dream.

The vision blurred and faded and redrew itself as an underground circus. Me, Max and Jim were reunited. They were no longer pecans nuts but Louis and Crimson were nowhere to be seen…

There was a uni-cycling elephant, oinker heads being fired from a cannon and a team of flying letter *V's*. Are these the *V's* Jim saw? If they were would they change into bees? This made me think… what else has Jim seen? What other dangers await us…

"I'm not in this vision as I have more important things to do than visit a circus," announced Crimson. He was trying to show off but he knew what we were thinking (that he would die at WaterLoo).

"I don't understand this circus vision Louis and where are you?" I squeaked.

"The answers are becoming complicated," he replied.

"No there not," squawked Crimson.

"Yes they are," snapped Louis.

"It's obvious," gloated Crimson. We watched him brush himself down and sit on the higher level. He was happy enough but the problem with this crossbreed was he did not communicate. Will this lack of teamwork be his downfall, I wonder?

"We need to find a place to change these pecans back," sighed Louis. He sat by the higher level next to Crimson with his legs dangling over towards the tracks. I joined the pair of them and cried.

All that was left was us two mice and one crossbreed against the world. But what other horrors await us? Will I ever see Jim or Max again? I do in this vision but can I trust something I don't understand? Will I ever see a Eon, Grimley or a rat again? Will I understand Rat-Routes? And will I find my destiny even though I am unsure of what it is? Are Jim and I really going to become unpredictables? Are Louis and the Professor really to become reptiles of the swamps? Will Crimson fall at WaterLoo? Will we understand this Dark Energy that absorbs and controls our emotions? Or is it now just a mysterious wall in Bell-Sized Park! Will we find the Dark Matter juices to rescue our pecan friends? Will we understand what Dark Matter is? And will we halt the hamster control of London? There are so many questions and so little time to find the answers…

END OF VOLUME TWO

AJ Howard – Biography

I am from Raynes Park, a small town in south London, England. I gave up my career in advertising after winning a short story competition and this encouraged me to be the writer I am today. I have travelled throughout Europe, hitchhiked in America and been a cruise ship photographer in the Caribbean. I have taken varied career paths since and discovered the real people of this world are down-trodden, lowly paid or work like dogs and these brothers are the influences of my writing style. I am able to record, design, illustrate and define any subject in any format.

For more information please follow links to Amazon from my website

fatmousestudios.com

Louis the
Furred III
Angels with
Dirty Whiskers
AJ Howard

WARTHOGS © 2010

Amongst the living a leadership of Warthogs terrorise the day makers. With uncanny fixations and complex coded messages they force the weak humans to succumb to slavery. Embittered beliefs that a warrior will save the day the Warthog leader changes into human form to discourage hatred. Incorporating various short stories, the Owl Wizards embark on the salvation of society. Using magic and hallucinations, these nocturnal hunters plot again the regime…

– with illustrations and maps

Genre: Fantasy Age 12+

FAT MOUSE PRESENTS series © 2013

Fat Mouse introduces comic strips, puzzles and quizzes for youngsters that assist them to read and spell: No Berries Fool, PIWW, a Slice to Freedom and William the Conkerer are the comic strips. The puzzles consist of Mouse & Hamster code breaking (as featured in the Louis the Furred series) spot the difference and word searches. The quizzes test the kiddies on their understanding of the Bee Confused, the Cream, Louis the Furred and the Wildlife and Run stories.

2 x books

50 pages each

in colour

Genre: Humour / Fiction Age 5-10

28122818R00114

Made in the USA
Charleston, SC
01 April 2014